A
Seductive
Kiss

Anthologies

Twice the Temptation

Let's Get It On

Going to the Chapel

Welcome to Leo's

Della's House of Style

A
Seductive
Kiss

FRANCIS RAY

ST. MARTIN'S GRIFFIN
NEW YORK

Published in the United States by St. Martin's Griffin, an imprint of St. Martin's Publishing Group

www.stmartins.com

ISBN 978-0-312-53647-3 (mass market paperback)
ISBN 978-1-250-62406-2 (trade paperback)
ISBN 978-1-4668-0416-6 (ebook)

First St. Martin's Griffin Edition: 2020

10 9 8 7 6 5 4 3 2 1

Chapter 1

People thought Dianne Leigh Harrington had the world on her personal yo-yo string. Strikingly beautiful with an exquisite face the camera loved, she was known around the world as "The Face," the only model for the House of Harrington's print advertisements and lead model for their runway shows. She was on the A list, got into all the exclusive nightspots, was voted one of the beautiful people in *People* magazine, was sought after by some of the richest men in the world.

Those who thought she lived a fairy-tale life were wrong.

In a one-of-a-kind, haute couture, strapless, blush-pink evening gown created especially to show off her smooth bare shoulders, shapely curves, and long legs, from the side split to midthigh, Dianne sipped her vintage champagne in a quiet corner of the lavish Plaza Hotel suite, and fought not to sigh.

She was lonely. So what else was new?

Dianne could recall few occasions in her life when she had truly felt happy and wanted. Tonight, with her two closest friends in the room, should have been one of those rare occasions. It wasn't. She felt too much like the odd man out, just as she had always been.

So she did what she always did when she felt left out: smiled, sipped her drink, and pretended she didn't have a care in the world. Too bad it wasn't true.

She should be content for once to observe rather than be observed. But the more she watched the obviously in love couples circulate around the suite, the lonelier she became. Because, just like always, tonight when the party was over she'd go home alone.

While she enjoyed her glamorous career as a model and spokeswoman for the House of Harrington, and visited some of the most fascinating cities in the world, she wanted more out of life. She was frequently in the company of other models or people in the fashion industry. They tended to go out in groups, but before the night was over they usually paired up with someone in the group or with someone they'd met. Dianne wasn't into casual affairs, so she always ended up alone.

The couples in the room had what she'd longed for all her life: unconditional love. She wasn't jealous, she just wanted what they had, wondered what it felt like to be totally loved and wanted.

As an only child, she'd been barely tolerated by her self-absorbed parents. Her mother, beautiful, elegant, and always perfect, was a slave to fashion. Her handsome father's unrelenting passion was golf. They looked good together, and freely enjoyed being the recipients of the Harrington fashion fortune. Neither would have dreamed of working. If they thought about Dianne at all, it was when it was convenient or when it made them look like the loving, charitable couple they pretended to be in public.

What a bunch of crock, Dianne thought as she took another sip. Her parents only loved themselves. They even bought their own Christmas presents since they reasoned that they knew what they wanted better than anyone. Dianne seldom made their Christmas list unless they hoped to gain from it somehow.

No matter how many years had passed, Dianne still thought of the Christmas Eve when she was five years old. With TV cameras rolling, her parents had made a very public display of donating her toys to those less fortunate. There had been no cameras the next morning when her mother presented herself with a flawless diamond necklace and earrings to match. Her father's gift to himself was a membership at one of the most exclusive golf clubs in the country.

Dianne shook the memory away. She was her own woman now. She had her beloved grandfather to thank for that. A sharp pain lanced through her. She still found it difficult to believe he'd been gone for four months. He'd believed in her. He hadn't thought she was too fat or too stupid for the D collection to be named for her. Both she and the line were instant hits. That had been fourteen long years ago. Modeling for Harrington was all she knew.

In the quiet of the night, that thought often frightened her. She should be able to do something beside strut down a runway, pose for a camera, and spout how fabulous these clothes made a woman look and feel.

Laughter brought her head up and around. Each

woman there had accomplished something in her own right. The men were just as successful. Her parents would have forgone anything to be there. The women were beautiful, the men gorgeous, but it was the unmistakable love in their eyes when they looked at each other that drew Dianne's attention, time and time again.

She was the only single woman there. She'd been invited by her best friend since childhood, Catherine Stewart Grayson, to help celebrate the successful closing of Sabra Raineau Grayson's Broadway play. She was Catherine's husband's sister-in-law. There was already talk that she would win another Tony for her role. She could add it to her growing collection of awards, including an Oscar. There had been a cast party last night but Pierce Grayson, Sabra's husband, wanted tonight to be just family and close friends.

In the room were Luke Grayson's brothers and sisters, their spouses, Sabra's sister, Laurel, and her new husband, Zach. Also in attendance were Shane Elliott and his wife, Paige, who was Zachary's sister. Looking uncomfortable but resigned in a tuxedo was Trent Masters with his famous wife, Dominique, Luke's cousin. They were all interrelated or friends. Luke's mother, Ruth, along with her brother and his wife, had already gone to their rooms. Dianne was the outsider as she'd always been.

Her slim fingers tightened on the stem of the flute, then eased. She wasn't going to feel sorry for herself. She wasn't the only single person there at least. Her gaze turned to the silent man across the room. She met

Rio's unflinching gaze. He simply watched her. To another person his unblinking gaze might have been unnerving, but she had grown up with parents who looked through her.

"You're all right?"

The sound of the rich baritone voice made her smile. Dianne turned, aware she'd see Alex Stewart, the only other unattached male in the room. Catherine's big brother had been the extra-special bonus of having her for a best friend. "Of course," she said, still smiling up at him. It had always been easy to talk with Alex. He had also been her first crush.

"Good," he said, staring down at her with his handsome, serious butterscotch-hued face. He had thick lashes her friends would kill for, a straight nose, and a mobile, sensual mouth that she had been wondering how it would feel against her own mouth entirely too much lately. "You're here to have fun."

Dragging her gaze away from his lips, Dianne thought of the issue at hand. Alex had always looked after her. Somehow he'd always known what to do to make her feel better. She wondered if he could give her what she needed this time as well.

She wanted a man to look at her as if she were his world, as if she made his life better. She realized she wanted that man to be Alex. The realization didn't surprise her. Somehow she knew he'd be a gentle, considerate lover. He was steady and dependable. He would also be discreet, another of her requirements.

Too many times she'd heard men brag about a

conquest when the relationship ended. Some of her women associates shrugged it off. Dianne knew she wouldn't be so blasé. It would wound her deeply. Outwardly she might look secure. She wasn't. Growing up, she'd been told too many times by her parents how utterly worthless she was.

Alex didn't think so, she thought, as she gazed up at him through a sweep of her lashes. But was he the man who could ease the ache in her heart and soul?

Alex stared down into the pensive, beautiful face of his one weakness, Dianne Harrington. He'd probably started falling in love with her the Christmas morning she was five years old and he was nine. He'd seen her crying on her porch steps because her parents had given away all her toys and Santa hadn't left any to replace them. He'd quickly climbed off his new bike and made up a story about Santa leaving the wrong-sized bike at his house.

The wide-eyed happy smile on her tearstained face had been worth the lie. He'd happily pushed her around on his bike most of the morning; the next day, using his own money that he'd saved for a telescope, he'd purchased her a pink bicycle. He couldn't explain to his parents why it had been important to use his own money, it just had been. They hadn't asked any more questions, just told him how proud of him they were.

He'd long since accepted that he could only have Dianne as a friend. If she learned how he felt, it would be awkward for her and embarrassing for him. Dianne was like a star, to be gazed at and admired but not touched.

"We're the only two unattached people here," Dianne said, watching Alex over the rim of her flute. "You think they're trying to tell us something?"

Alex, used to Dianne's flirtatious ways, nodded toward Rio, his face blank, leaning against the wall. Dianne followed the direction of Alex's gaze. Rio was gorgeous, and beneath his expertly cut tux he probably had a body that would make a woman drool, but there was also a dangerous alertness about him. She could never be completely comfortable around him the way she could be with Alex. "Not my type," she said.

Alex's brows knitted. There was something different about her tonight. He'd watched her from a distance, a lifelong habit, most of the evening. There was a sad wistfulness in her face that he'd caught glimpses of more and more that evening. Dianne was usually the life of the party, joking, laughing. Tonight she had been quiet and remained apart.

"You're sure everything is all right with the House of Harrington?" he asked.

Dianne accepted that Alex had always been able to read her better than anyone, even Catherine. "Fine. I guess I'm just tired. My plane got in from Paris this afternoon."

His long-fingered hand brushed up and down her bare arm, sending shivers in its wake. "Are you concerned about meeting with the new CEO?" Alex asked, apparently unwilling to let it go.

The smile on Dianne's face vanished. The House of Harrington's board had elected a new CEO a month ago to take her grandfather's place. She swallowed the lump in her throat. Her grandfather had been the only relative who saw her as a person and not as a paycheck. "No," she finally answered.

Alex's frown didn't clear. "With your grandfather gone, you need a contract."

"My parents still have a controlling interest in Harrington. We both know money rules them." She tried to say the words carelessly but, from the concerned way Alex looked at her, he knew how much it still bothered her that her parents didn't love her.

"I could clear my schedule and go with you," he offered.

Alex was watching out for her. Again. He'd do it and think nothing of it. Too many times to count, Alex had been there for her when she was growing up. "You're a great friend," she said, and watched something flicker in his beautiful black eyes.

"I'll always be there for you, you know that," he said softly.

She did. Alex was solid. He worked with one of the top law firms in New York, and was in line to be a partner. He had a Who's Who list of clients, but he also took on pro-bono cases. Catherine had mentioned that he and his two best friends in New York were known as the renegades because they followed their own dictates. They cared about people more than the bottom line. Right, not money, ruled them.

But was the possibility of being the sole object of his

affection for a short time worth the loss of his friendship when it was over? And it would end eventually. She wasn't lovable.

Perhaps it was in her genetic makeup, or perhaps it was that she wasn't the sharpest knife in the drawer. As her mother had pointed out more than once, if she hadn't been the face of Harrington, there was no telling what would have become of her. Her mother, a former runway model, had managed to marry the son and only child of the founders of the House of Harrington, Aaron and Nora Harrington, before she turned twenty-three.

Dianne had no romantic prospects. There were men who wanted to have sex with her because of who she was or the way she looked or just to say they had, but none who wanted *her*, the woman behind "The Face." She didn't know why she felt tears prick her eyes. She bent to place her glass on the nearby table.

Alex felt a mild panic on seeing the sheen of tears in Dianne's eyes. Lawyers didn't panic. Without counting the cost, he pulled her into his arms. "Whatever it is, I'm here." The warmth of her body against his, the soft sigh, made his unsteady heart beat out a warning, which he ignored.

His hand splayed in the middle of her bare back. Her skin was softer than velvet, smooth as silk. Heat and desire swept though him. He held her closer. There wasn't anything he wouldn't risk for this woman, even his foolish heart.

In Alex's arms, Dianne felt safe, wanted. She'd experienced that emotion pitifully few times in her life.

Reluctantly she pushed against the rock-hard chest and stared up into the face of the one man besides her grandfather she'd always been comfortable with.

At the moment, Alex's dark brows were furrowed with concern, his piercing black eyes narrowed intently on her face. He cared. She could build on that if she dared. But she'd always been a coward; she'd been hurt too many times when she reached out, especially to her parents.

"I guess I'm still tired from my flight today." She tried to smile, but for once her facial muscles refused to obey. "I think I'll call it a night." For a tense moment, she thought he would question her further.

"Let's say good night and I'll see you home," he said.

Persistent, stubborn, loyal. There wasn't a better man in the world than Alex. "Thanks, but I can see myself home. You aren't leaving your family and friends."

The long, elegant fingers of his right hand brushed down the bare slope of her shoulder. "You're like family."

The hot shivers that raced through her at his casual touch were at odds with his statement. She'd once thought she'd like to be a member of the loving, happy Stewart family, but she was suddenly glad she wasn't.

"You can see me to a cab." Pleased her voice wasn't as breathless as she felt, she went to say good night to the others in the room, all the time very much aware of the solid warmth of Alex directly behind her. She couldn't recall ever being so aware of him. She didn't know if it was because of her thoughts about the possibility of them becoming lovers or something else.

"Thanks for the invitation, Catherine," Dianne said to her oldest and dearest friend. She wasn't sure how her childhood would have turned out if not for the connection she'd made with Catherine and Alex. "I had a wonderful time."

"I'm glad you could come," Catherine said, hugging Dianne. Glamorous and beautiful, Catherine wore an emerald-green gown that showed off her slender figure. "I wish we weren't leaving so early in the morning so we'd have time to get together."

"Me too," Dianne said, swallowing the lump in her throat. It had been six months since they'd seen each other in person. Since Dianne's plane had gotten in so late, they'd had only a short time to talk tonight. "The next break I get, look for me on your doorstep."

"I'm holding you to that," Catherine said, holding Dianne's hands in hers.

"You're always welcome," Luke, Catherine's husband, said as he slipped his arms around her waist. "Anytime."

"Thank you." Dianne leaned over to whisper in an aside, "You definitely picked a winner."

"Don't I know it, but he wasn't easy." Catherine laughed.

Luke chuckled. "You had me from the moment you got the drop on me with the semiautomatic."

Those around them laughed as well. Luke had surprised Catherine at his cabin, and she'd greeted him with a gun. "That's my girl, always cool and in control," Dianne said.

Catherine and Luke shared a look. "Because of Luke," she whispered, and leaned into his muscular body.

"Thank God," Dianne said. Luke had rescued Catherine in more ways than one. Hugging both Luke and Catherine, she said her good-byes to the others in the room, then left with Alex.

Instead of taking her arm, he slung his arm around her shoulders. He'd done it a hundred times, but tonight she wanted to lean into him.

"The family is going to spend Thanksgiving again this year with Catherine and Luke's family in Santa Fe. You know you have a standing invitation," Alex said.

Where she'd be the outsider. Her grandfather hadn't been much on holidays since her grandmother had died when Dianne was eighteen. Last Thanksgiving she'd been stranded in the airport due to a snowstorm. Her Thanksgiving dinner had been a sandwich out of a vending machine while sitting in a hard plastic chair surrounded by strangers. By the time she'd finally arrived back in New York, she had to fly out again for a shoot in Hawaii. She punched the elevator button. "Thanks, I'll check my schedule."

"Why don't I believe you?"

The elevator doors slid open. She stepped in and punched the lobby button. "You're a lawyer," she said, tossing him a teasing grin.

He didn't smile back. "How about lunch tomorrow? You can tell me about the latest doings in the fashion world."

She glanced up at him through a flirtatious sweep of lashes, aware this time she was doing it on purpose. Although she had an apartment in New York, she was seldom there because she traveled so much for fashion shoots, runway shows, and appearances, or was at their Paris location.

She could count on one hand the number of times in the past year she had spent more than thirty minutes at a time with Alex. One or the other, usually her, was always busy. But she always made a point of calling him whenever she was in town.

The elevator opened and they stepped off. "Your schedule is just as hectic as mine," she said as they crossed the immense lobby. Overhead, huge Waterford crystal chandeliers glittered.

"How does noon at Le Cirque sound?" he asked as they went through the revolving door and outside. "Taxi, please," he told the doorman.

Le Cirque was usually booked days in advance. "You're going to ditch a client?" she asked.

"Not necessary," he smiled, showing dimples that made him look like an adorable little boy. "You forget. I know people."

She had forgotten, probably because, unlike a lot of people she associated with, Alex wasn't a show-off. He was one of those self-assured men who were comfortable with who they were. He didn't have to prove anything to anyone.

He came from a very wealthy and influential family. His father was a successful third-generation banker. His mother was a renowned California senator. His younger sister, Catherine, was a well-respected child psychologist, a past professor at Stanford, and a *New York Times* best-selling children's author. If that wasn't enough, her husband Luke's cousin, Daniel Falcon, was enormously wealthy, and Luke's baby sister was married to real estate billionaire Blade Navarone.

But Alex wasn't a man to trade on the wealth and fame of others. He didn't have to. He was wealthy and respected in his own right. Unlike her father, Alex didn't use his power for his own selfish gain, and thus, when he sought people's help, they responded favorably.

The cab pulled up to the curb in front of them. She stole another look at Alex. Her heart made that crazy knock in her chest again. There wasn't a shred of doubt in her mind that he'd fulfill her every sexual fantasy and then some.

But was a brief, hot affair worth losing his friendship? "Why don't I take a rain check and get back to you after I've had a chance to rest?"

She easily read the disappointment on his face. She masked her own disappointment. She liked being with him.

"All right. You have my numbers if you change your mind." He opened the taxi's rear door and waited until she was seated. " 'Night. Don't forget to take some fluids before you go to bed."

She smiled. Alex was one of a kind. It would be difficult if not impossible to find another man who excited her like he did, and who always thought of her well-being. "I won't. Good night, Alex."

Shutting the door, he straightened. The cab pulled

off. Through the rear window Dianne watched Alex, gorgeous and elegant, until traffic obscured him. She wondered if she had enough courage to proposition her best friend's brother to be her lover.

Chapter 2

After a restless night, Dianne decided to take Alex from the top of her list. For all she knew, her body's unusual reaction to his was an anomaly. What she needed to do was go out with a few other men and see if it happened again.

With that thought in mind, she took a seat on the curved white leather sofa in the spacious living area of her apartment and spread out the business cards she'd collected on her last trip to New York three months before. It had only been for a weekend to attend a charity dinner for Helping Hands, a nonprofit organization she and her grandfather supported.

She'd gone by herself and had been swamped with men wanting to take her out. She'd refused all of them. With her grandfather gone only a month, she'd felt even less like dating than usual.

Now, with the bright morning sun streaming through the windows behind her and one leg tucked beneath her hips, Dianne leaned over to study the nine cards spread out on the glass-topped coffee table. The room, done completely in white with splashes of red and green, was restful, but although she'd lived there for three years she still didn't feel as if it was home. Then again, no place ever had, not even while she'd lived with her grandfather.

She took a sip of her spring water with a twist of lime. Orange juice or a smoothie would have tasted better and perhaps appeased the gnawing hunger, but she had less than two weeks to lose ten pounds. She'd tried to pinch an inch at her waist that morning while in the shower and thankfully couldn't.

No matter. René, the exacting head designer at Harrington's Paris headquarters, had a screaming fit when she'd gone in on Friday to try on the clothes for the new winter line. He'd adamantly refused to even let her see the clothes, declaring they wouldn't fit, and ordered her to lose ten pounds before he saw her again. Since she loved food, losing ten pounds in such a short amount of time was going to be a challenge.

But she'd faced challenges before—like the one at hand.

Placing the glass on a leather coaster, she brought her mind back to the current situation, selecting a man to see if he could make her skin tingle and her heart race. If so, she'd consider him to be The One.

Studying the business cards, she moved two aside. One was another model. The second belonged to an agent who represented several models. She demanded discretion, and that meant she didn't want anyone remotely associated with the fashion industry. Despite modeling all over the world, being in front of the camera, and doing countless TV shows and interviews, she remained a very private person.

Another card joined the two. She recalled that the banker had had a faint circular line on his ring finger. He might have been recently divorced, but she wasn't taking the chance.

Six cards were left. She tried to recall what the six men looked like, got faint images, but they kept slipping away and Alex would stand there, looking good enough to make her sigh and squirm.

"Concentrate, Dianne." She picked up a card, reached for the phone, and dialed. She'd never asked a man out on a date or propositioned one. She figured once they knew who she was, they'd take over.

"Hello."

Dianne came upright at the sound of the woman's voice. She looked at the card. "I'm sorry. I must have dialed incorrectly."

"What number did you dial?"

Dianne didn't see what difference that made, but repeated the number, ending by saying, "I'm sorry. I was looking for Isaac."

A string of curses singed Dianne's ear. "That lying, cheating bastard. I knew if I had his cell phone he'd trip himself up. Isaac's my man and—"

"Sorry. Good-bye." Dianne quickly hung up, leaned back against the back of the sofa, then came upright when she remembered caller ID. She slumped back again. Her number was blocked. Isaac was certainly in for it when he saw that woman again, but if she thought he was cheating and still calling him *her man,* he would probably talk his way out of it.

Alex would never cheat on her. *Concentrate. Alex is not in the equation.*

Briefly closing her eyes, Dianne picked up another card. Surely a Wall Street broker was honest. She thought of all the recent insider-trading scandals and almost put his card back. She didn't because she'd heard so many horrific lies about models sleeping around and doing drugs. She dialed the number.

"Reginald Hall. Can I help you?"

His voice didn't do anything for her, but perhaps when she saw him she'd get that tingling sensation she'd felt last night looking at Alex. "Mr. Hall, Reginald, this is Dianne Harrington." When she paused and he didn't say anything, she became a bit unsure and continued. "We met at the Helping Hands charity dinner. You asked me out."

He chuckled. "Sorry, sweetheart. You're too late. I got engaged last weekend."

She stunk at finding a man. "I'm sorry to trouble you. Please accept my best wishes for a long and happy marriage."

"She's a Butler of the Southampton Butlers. My future and happiness are assured. Good-bye."

Frowning, Dianne hung up again. He'd sounded as if, because the bride's family was extremely wealthy, his happiness was a foregone conclusion. He hadn't even mentioned the bride's happiness. Obviously, he was thinking of money and not his bride. Sad.

Dianne frowned at the four remaining cards, shoved them with the blunt tip of her lacquered pink nails, and contemplated which one to call next. Businessman, real estate executive, lawyer, marketing executive.

The phone on the end table rang, causing her to jump. What if the angry wife or girlfriend had somehow managed to get her phone number? Cautiously, Dianne peered over the rounded arm of the sofa to look at the caller ID: JENKINS AND HOPKINS LAW FIRM. Alex. For some odd reason she felt guilty, as if she had somehow betrayed him.

She chewed on her bottom lip, considered letting the call go to voice mail. If she did that, he'd worry. Slowly, she picked up the receiver. "Hello," she said, her voice coming out a bit breathless.

"Dianne. Did I catch you at a bad time?" Alex asked.

"No. No." She rushed to reassure him. "I'm fine. Just going over some things."

"That's why I called. To check on you," he explained. "How did you sleep?"

"Fine," she lied, reasoning it wouldn't do any good to tell him that thoughts of him, either locked in a passionate embrace or avoiding her after their affair ended badly, had kept her up most of the night.

"You don't sound fine," Alex said. "I just wanted you to know that if you change your mind about lunch today, we still have a table, but maybe you should take it easy. Perhaps we could go out tomorrow."

If only she could take the chance. Dianne glanced at the business cards. "My plans are kind of fluid."

"I understand. I better let you get some rest. Bye."
His voice lost some of the brightness she'd become so
accustomed to hearing.

"Bye, Alex, and thanks for calling." She hung up
and reached for the card of the lawyer. Perhaps if she
couldn't have one, she could be content with another.

Alex hung up and tried to keep the picture of Dianne in
bed with another man at bay. He couldn't. She'd sounded
breathless, nervous. Usually when they talked there was
no hesitation, as there had been just now.

Unable to sit, he rose from his desk to stare out the
window behind him. He'd had a corner office for the
two past years, and usually enjoyed the view of Man-
hattan. Not today. He was too stricken with images that
twisted his gut.

Perhaps he should have made his move long ago. He
hadn't because he knew she thought of him as the big
brother of her best friend, and as someone she could talk
to when things became tough. She needed that given her
worthless parents. Blowing out a breath, he took his seat
and pulled a client's file in front of him.

He'd learned early there was no sense living in the
past or thinking about what might have been. You took
your best shot at life, gave it your all. He only had to
look at the picture of his parents with Catherine and
him on his first day at the law firm to reaffirm that no-
tion. They'd flown up to surprise him. The picture in a
crystal frame arrived a week later. It had been their way
of telling him they would always be there for him no

matter how far away he might be, but also that life wasn't always easy.

His mother and sister had fought discrimination every step of their professional career climb. They'd never complained; as they'd both said, what good would it have done. They'd simply shown those who didn't believe they were capable of being a US senator for California or a professor of psychology at Stanford that they were wrong.

The phone on his desk rang. He punched the intercom. "Yes, Alice."

"Mr. Sinclair is here."

"Send him in." Alex came to his feet just as Payton "Sin" Sinclair came through the door. Six foot three of lean, conditioned muscles, Sin wore his usual grin. Dressed in a Tom Ford single-button gray suit, he looked like the successful businessman he was. But he was just as much at ease in jeans and worn cowboy boots. The problems of life seldom got to Sin. His comment was that it wasted time and solved nothing. "Sin, how many millions did you make today?"

Deep, roguish laughter erupted as ebony eyes danced with mischief. "It's only half past nine."

"And you work sixteen-hour days," Alex said. Sin was a sports consultant, and the best in the business. When companies wanted to align themselves with sports figures and owners, the go-to man was Sinclair. He had the boundless energy of a two-year-old and the tenacity of a pit bull. He was outrageously creative and street-smart.

"Sleeping, I might miss something," Sin came back.

Since Alex worked long hours as well, he understood Sin's strong work ethic. Waving his friend to a seat in front of his desk, Alex leaned against it and crossed his arms. "How long will you be in town this time?" he asked. Sin had an eighty-person agency with offices in Dallas, Chicago, Charlotte, Phoenix, and Los Angeles.

"A couple of weeks. I'm working a deal."

"When aren't you working a deal?"

A devilish grin flashed across his handsome, bearded face. "And you and C. J. benefit with tickets to the top sports events in the city," Sin reminded Alex. "Baseball season is soon winding down and football is gearing up. We'd miss you."

Alex barely kept from wincing. He might not go out much, but he loved sports. "You know how to make a point."

"So I've been told. We're still on for our monthly pool game Friday?" Sin leaned back in the chair, linked his slim fingers over his flat stomach, and crossed his long legs.

Alex hesitated, thought of Dianne, and took a seat behind his desk. "I'm not sure. I might be busy."

Sin's eyes narrowed. Slowly, he came upright. "Your business calendar is always three weeks out. It must be personal. Who is she? Is she beautiful?"

"No one you'd know," Alex said. *Sin* wasn't Sinclair's nickname for nothing.

"Possessive, not a good sign," Sin teased, punctuating his words with a firm shake of his head. "You're too young to be tied down to one woman."

If only. "We're just friends."

Sin blew out an impatient breath. "If I had a dollar every time I've heard a man say those words, I could retire early."

"You tried that five years ago after you sold your online marketing firm. You became bored within two months," Alex said, relieved to have a chance to change the subject. "Now you're king of consulting in the sports world."

"What can I say, I like challenges. Speaking of which, I finally cinched the deal with Cameron Mc-Bride for Umps energy drink. The contracts will arrive by messenger this morning for you to look over."

"I'll have my secretary watch for them."

"Good." Sin came to his feet and glanced at his platinum watch with six time zones. "One more thing. From personal experience, teaching a woman to play pool can be a satisfying experience."

The image that jumped into Alex's mind—standing behind Dianne, her hips pressed against him as he bent over her—was titillating, but it would never happen. "Talk to you later, Sin."

"I can take a hint." Sin went to the door. "One thing I learned in this business that you might want to consider: If you don't get into the game, you can't win. Bye."

Alex was not the impulsive type. He thought things through and always went with what was safe, responsible. So why was he getting out of a cab in front of Dianne's apartment building instead of his?

Good question. If only he had a good answer.

He stepped onto the sidewalk. He'd tried to talk himself out of coming here, but he'd been unable to. Sin was right. If Alex didn't at least try to see if Dianne was attracted to him, he had no one to blame except himself if she ended up with another man. The buzz he'd gotten last night when he touched her was expected; her response wasn't.

They'd been together hundreds of time, touched a thousand times, but last night it had been different. She must have felt it.

If he hadn't gotten those sexual vibrations, he would be at home going over Sin's contracts, which he hadn't been able to finish at work. He often took work home. He wasn't much for going out. It was another strike against things working out between him and Dianne. She liked going out. The last weekend she'd been in town, she hadn't been home one night.

He stared up at the towering apartment complex whose prices started at three million and rose sharply from there. He shouldn't be here, but he didn't seem to be able to stay away. He made his feet move to the glass-and-brass door.

"Good evening, sir." Tipping his hat-covered head, the doorman opened the door.

"Evening," Alex said and entered the fashionable lobby with large framed and signed art, modern furniture groupings, and potted plants. He headed for the elevators and pushed the button for twenty-two. And waited. When he saw her he'd—

The elevator doors slid open. His thoughts slammed to a halt.

"Alex. What a surprise," Truss Martin said, a wide smile on his too-handsome face.

With difficulty Alex dragged his gaze from Dianne, who was looking beautiful and tempting in a short ice-blue evening dress, to Truss, a lawyer and fellow Racquetball Club member. Truss was a hard-nosed corporate attorney with a bit of a reputation as a ladies' man.

Alex moved aside for them and other people getting off the elevator, and hoped his lawyer face was firmly in place. "Hello, Truss. Dianne."

"Hello, Alex," Dianne finally murmured. Her gaze kept slipping away from his face.

Truss frowned, looking from one to the other. "I guess you two know each other."

The question of how well hung in the air. "Dianne is my sister's best friend. I just came by to see how she was feeling. Obviously, it wasn't necessary."

Dianne jerked her head up, her gaze narrowed. Had he been accusatory?

He probably shouldn't care, but facing the reality of Dianne with someone else was a kick in the gut. "Well, good night, and have a great time."

Dianne wanted to go after Alex. Explain somehow. But what could she say? *I wanted to see if another man could turn me on the way you did*?

"Were you two an item?" Truss asked.

"No." Dianne faced her date with a smile. There had been countless times she hadn't felt like being "on," so she'd learned early to mask her true feelings. "I've known Alex since I was five. He watched over both his sister and me for so long, it's a habit. I was feeling the effects of jet lag yesterday, and he was worried."

Truss stared at Alex as he left the lobby. "I'm not sure that's all he feels."

Dianne's heart thumped. Maybe—

"Let's get going before they give our table away, and then we're going to the theater."

"Wonderful," Dianne said, but she didn't feel wonderful. The last thing she wanted to do was hurt Alex. Yet she had a feeling that was exactly what she had just done.

Chapter 3

After leaving Dianne's apartment building, Alex hailed a taxi. This time he knew exactly where he was heading. "Callahan's on Ninety-fifth Street," he instructed the driver.

Alex's hands clenched and unclenched. He felt like he'd been run over by a semi. Had Truss been with her that morning? Were they lovers? He couldn't think about them being intimate. If he did, he'd tell the cabdriver to take him back to Dianne's apartment to mess up Truss's pretty face.

"Ten dollars and fifty cents."

Giving the man a twenty, Alex quickly got out of the cab. He didn't stop until he was sitting at the bar. Even on a Monday night, Callahan's was crowded. C. J. had taken over the bar that his uncle had left to him and turned it into a favorite watering hole of people in the area.

"Hi, Alex," greeted Mary, one of the three regular bartenders. "I'll get your beer in a minute."

"Scotch. Straight."

Mary paused, stared at him. It was on the tip of his

tongue to ask if he'd stuttered. Instead he braced his arms on the polished cherrywood surface. He wasn't going to be one of those people who took their anger out on everyone around them.

The squat glass hit the counter in front of him. Alex picked up the glass and saw C. J. He was six-four of solid muscle. He could be a hard man if crossed. He was wealthy enough to run the bar as a hobby to keep the promise to his long-dead uncle, but he was business-savvy enough to make it turn a tidy profit. C. J. was a man you could count on. "Working the bar tonight?"

"Looks like."

Alex tilted the glass, felt the scotch burn all the way down. The empty glass hit the counter. He still felt like crap. "Another."

C. J. didn't move, just looked at Alex with those piercing light brown eyes of his that saw too much. "Is she worth it?"

"I came here for a scotch, not conversation."

"You came here to forget, but I can tell you from the experience of my ill-spent youth that when you wake up in the morning, whatever it is will still be eating at you." C. J. picked up the glass and walked away. Seconds later he returned with two longnecks expertly held between his fingers. "Back booth."

Alex could leave, find another bar, and have as many scotches as he wanted. The back booth meant conversation. He didn't want to talk. He wanted . . . He wanted Dianne.

Sliding off the stool, Alex went to the back booth. C. J. was already there. Alex heard the crack of the pool

balls mixed with the ding of the arcade in the area behind him. Taking a seat, he wrapped his hands around
the cold bottle in front of him. "I could blame this on
Sin for giving me hope that I had a chance."

"Sin is behind this?" C. J. asked with a frown.

"No." Alex took a sip of beer. "He was trying to help.
Bottom line is I choked and lost the only woman for
me."

"She's engaged and getting married tomorrow?"

Alex's brows bunched. "No."

Lifting his beer, C. J. took a sip. "Then I'd say you're
hitting the bottle a bit prematurely. A smart lawyer like
you should have figured that out."

"I figured out long ago she wasn't for me. Guess I
forgot." Alex's hands gripped the bottle, then he took a
sip. "I went over to her place tonight to check on her
and she was going out with another lawyer who be-
longs to my Racquetball Club."

C. J. leaned over and looked at Alex's hands, then
leaned back. "I see your parents' excellent training came
through and you didn't deck him."

"She would have still been with him, probably hov-
ering over him as the police carted me off to jail," Alex
said tightly.

"But you would have felt better and not regretted
taking the shot when you had the chance."

Alex shook his head. "You know, you're downright
scary at times."

"Who is she? And why am I just hearing about her?"

Alex didn't expect C. J. to acknowledge his uncanny
way of reading people. They'd known each other since

Alex had moved into his building eight years ago. C. J. had helped the inept movers, then invited Alex to Callahan's for a beer. They'd clicked and become close friends, along with C. J.'s best friend, Sin, who lived on the top floor in the penthouse.

"Dianne Harrington, a high-fashion international model better known as 'The Face' for the House of Harrington. She spends a lot of time in Europe. Has a place in Paris," Alex said. "She and Catherine have been friends since they were five."

"I've seen her."

Alex wasn't surprised. C. J.'s family had a lot of business interests. His mother was highly connected socially. When she made him feel guilty enough, he attended a few high-society events. Alex preferred staying at home with a good book or watching the stars with his telescope.

"Nice legs."

Alex's eyes narrowed. "Watch it."

"Would you prefer I said she was dog-ugly?"

All Alex could do was shake his head. "You know, you're crazy."

"Nope. I just say what's on my mind while other people think about saying it." C. J. took a sip of his beer.

"You went home to see your parents this weekend," Alex guessed. C. J.'s parents had a home in East Hampton. So did C. J.'s older brother, his wife, and their two children. C. J. didn't drink while working, but he'd drunk more beer than Alex had.

"Absence definitely does not make the heart grow fonder," he finally answered.

"Because you're so stubborn. Your parents love you. So does your brother and his family. You love them, too." Alex leaned back in the booth. "You're just annoyed because you'll have to wear a suit and tie every day instead of a T-shirt and jeans."

C. J. made a rumbling sound. "Don't remind me. If only my brother and Dad didn't have health problems, and my brother didn't have to retire early."

"Understandable. A heart attack and quadruple bypass at fifty would make any sensible man take a long hard look at his life."

"But why mess up mine in the process?" C. J. practically snarled.

"Running Callahan Software full-time will be different than a bar, but you'll handle it just as you've expertly handled everything else in your life." Alex nudged his beer aside and stood. "I'm going home."

C. J. grabbed both bottles by the neck and came to his feet. "You didn't get in that corner office by giving up without a fight. Go after her if you want her."

"Everything isn't always so cut and dried," Alex said.

"It is if you make it that way." C. J. lifted the bottles. "Bring 'The Face' over one night, and the first one is on the house. I want to see if my memory of her legs is on target."

Alex pushed C. J.'s broad shoulder playfully, chuckled, and put a twenty in C. J.'s pocket. "Talking was better than the booze. Later."

"Later, man. My money's on you." C. J. held up the bottles. "Remember, we have a reputation to uphold. A renegade wouldn't let another man take his woman."

Alex's features hardened. His eyes chilled.

"Keep that anger; remember the churning in your gut. Go get your woman."

"I'm not you," Alex said.

"Be thankful." C. J. stepped closer. "I've seen you in your full lawyer mode. You're cool, unflappable. You're prepared when you walk into that courtroom or into mediation. You saved Callahan Software a butt-load of money in that copyright infringement case. You've kept Sin out of court with your airtight contracts. Now use that same sharp mind to prepare a strategy to win your woman."

"Telephone, C. J." the bartender called over the loud noise.

"Probably my mother or my brother. I'm supposed to be interviewing an executive assistant, for goodness' sake," C. J. said.

"Why not keep Paul's?" Alex asked.

"Because the sneaky Heath, who's running things until I get there, already asked for her and Paul agreed. I don't want an executive assistant; I want to run my bar in peace."

"I don't think you have a choice."

"You want to trade lives?" C. J. suggested, and Alex wasn't so sure he was kidding.

"No." Alex folded his arms.

"Some friend you are. And here I was going to tell you to bring 'The Face' over on Friday."

"Sin beat you to it, but I'll be watching both of you if we come," Alex said. "Women fall over themselves for you."

He grinned. "They do, don't they?"

Alex felt a smile tug the corner of his mouth. "Go answer the phone."

C. J.'s smile vanished. "I was trying to ignore it."

"Drinking won't solve my problem, and neither will ignoring your family solve yours," Alex told him.

"But it will make me feel better."

With one final friendly pat on C. J.'s broad shoulder, Alex left the bar and headed down the street to his place. Maybe C. J. and Sin were right. Perhaps he should go after her. They certainly knew more about women than he did. Alex wasn't a monk, but his focus had been work, specifically making partner by the time he was forty. Perhaps it was time for that to change . . . if it wasn't too late.

He'd call her tomorrow and try to get a feel if she was serious about Truss or just dating. Standing back certainly hadn't gained him anything. He'd invite her to Callahan's for a friendly game of pool for a start. And when they went, C. J. better not look at her legs.

Dianne tried to have a good time with Truss, she really did. Truss was a wonderful conversationalist, courteous, and good looking. But his touch didn't make her shiver and ache.

She'd made the discovery with the first touch of his hand on her bare arm when they walked from her apartment to the elevator. Except for the warmth of his hand, he might as well have been a mannequin.

She'd thought perhaps it might happen if he held her. But when his arm curved lightly around her waist on the short walk to the taxicab, it was the same. Warmth and nothing else.

Later that evening, staring across a candlelit table into each other's eyes proved just as big of a zero. The food was delicious, the restaurant elegant and quiet. It should have been the perfect place to start a relationship. Perhaps it would have been if even a tiny spark were there and, more to the point, if she didn't keep seeing the hurt on Alex's face.

She would have asked Truss to take her back to her apartment after dinner if not for the sold-out Broadway play Truss said he was anxious to see. The theme of unrequited love made her feel more alone, and guilty for being there with him. The woman sitting next to him should have made the evening more enjoyable for him and not wasted his time or his money.

Arriving back at her apartment after the play, she opened the door and stuck out her hand. She wasn't going to take the chance that he might want to kiss her good night. "Thank you, Truss. I had a wonderful time."

His smile was off center. "Something tells me you would have had a better time with Alex. Am I right?"

She didn't know how to respond.

"He's a lucky man." Shaking her hand, Truss headed for the elevator.

Inside her apartment, Dianne undressed, took a long bath, then discovered she was too restless to sleep. She felt guilty about the horrible date with Truss, worried about Alex. Getting up, she turned on the lamp by her bed and went to stare into the mirror over the dresser.

She didn't see any dark circles under her eyes, but she would if she continued to have problems sleeping.

That mustn't happen. She didn't want to face René with the extra pounds *and* dark circles. Makeup could mask the dark circles, but she'd rather not give René anything else to ream her out about.

She glanced at the clock on the night chest: 1:33 AM. She bit her lower lip and stared at the phone beside the clock. She wanted to call Alex, but he was probably asleep. If he did answer, what would she say? *I foolishly went out on a date to find a man who made my heart race and my skin tingle the same way you do, and learned that you're the only man who can make me feel that way—and you're off limits.*

Or was he?

She could sit there all night worrying, or she could take the chance. Before her courage failed her, she picked up the phone and dialed. It was answered on the second ring.

"Hello."

Had he been unable to sleep as well? "Hi, Alex. I know it's late, but . . ." Her voice trailed off.

"Dianne, are you all right?"

"I'm fine." She wrapped her arm around her waist. "It was nice of you to check on me."

"Did you and Truss have a good time?"

She didn't know if she heard criticism in his question or not. "I didn't. He probably didn't, either."

"What happened? Did he get out of line? I—"

"No, he was a gentleman." She ran her fingers through

her hair. "That was the first time we went out. I thanked him with a handshake. There weren't any sparks."

"You want sparks?"

"Don't you?" she asked.

"One of my top five," he said, sounding more and more like the playful, dependable Alex.

She smiled and sat on the bed. "And the other four?"

"Secret. Do you think your fluid schedule will allow you to have lunch with me tomorrow?"

For once, Dianne, reach out for what you want. She wanted to be with Alex. "A definite possibility."

"I'll see you at twelve at Le Cirque. I've made arrangements for us to order from the private dining menu if you wish."

Alex certainly had the connections. "All right."

"And Dianne?"

"Yes?"

"Thanks for the call."

Feeling warm and happy, she curled in the bed. "You're welcome. 'Night, Alex."

" 'Night."

Hanging up, Dianne turned off the light and pulled the covers up to her shoulder. In a matter of seconds, she was asleep with a smile on her face.

Chapter 4

Dianne saw Alex when she was a few steps inside Le Cirque. Her heart knocked in her chest. Her hand clenched on the small clutch in her hand. He was sexy, elegant, and handsome. What woman wouldn't respond to him?

Their gazes met, clung. She felt an unfamiliar frisson of heat. The sensation surprised, then pleased her. The erratic heartbeat could be attributed to nerves. The heat couldn't.

If Alex was the one she decided to have her first affair with, she wanted to feel all the wonderful, giddy sensations she'd dreamed and read about and never experienced.

Crossing the room, seeing him come to his full height of six foot plus, the irrepressible warmth of his eyes on her, she felt her body heat even more. He was genuinely pleased to see her. He wasn't studying the circus-themed dining room in the contemporary French restaurant, examining the menu, or any of the other things he could have been doing in a place that catered to the visual and epicurean senses. His gaze had been fixed on the entrance. Somehow she knew he'd been anxiously waiting for her. Her explanation of jet lag hadn't thrown him off.

He worried and cared. They were great points to be considered when making her final decision. Or had she already made it?

"Hi, Alex," she said. "I hope I didn't keep you waiting."

"You're worth the wait," he said.

Dianne's eyes widened with pleasure and surprise. She'd worn a sunny yellow sheath that reached to midthigh, and four-inch heels in the hope of making just such an impression. Yet in all the years she had known Alex, he'd never done or said anything that indicated he thought of her as anything more than his sister's best friend.

From the startled, almost embarrassed look on his face, he was just as surprised. Perhaps she wouldn't have to work so hard to convince him to be the one. She smiled, her decision made. "Why, thank you." Dianne took her seat.

Taking his chair next to hers, Alex still looked a bit shocked by what he had said. "You must hear that a lot."

"I do, but it's usually from people saying what they think I want to hear. You're different." She picked up her menu. "Catherine called me this morning. She was bubbling as usual. She and Luke are so much in love."

Alex relaxed and picked up his menu as well. "She's happy. Luke is a great guy. So is his whole family."

"Welcome to Le Cirque. Would you like the sommelier or a glass of wine while you decide on your lunch selection?" asked the waiter with a delightful French accent.

"Tonic water," Dianne said, handing him the menu. "I already know I want a spinach salad with vinaigrette, if possible."

Accepting the menu, the gray-haired man smiled. "With pleasure," he said and turned to Alex. "And you, sir?"

"The same to drink, but I'll have the roasted beef fillet, fresh asparagus, and herb-roasted potatoes." Alex gave the man his menu. When he turned to leave, Alex said to Dianne, "You need to eat more."

"Not according to René."

Alex frowned. "Who's that?"

"The head designer at Harrington's in Paris," she told him as they were served their drinks. It still rankled. "He said . . ."

"What?" Alex leaned across the table, his gorgeous mouth set.

"That I needed to lose a few pounds," Diana admitted, hiding behind her glass. Only René hadn't put it so politely. He'd shouted at her, told her she'd ruin his fabulous designs. She had to lose ten pounds before she returned to Paris after the meeting on Monday.

She sighed. How could she lose that much weight in the time she had left? She certainly wasn't going to take some of the drastic steps the others models resorted to.

"The man is crazy. There's nothing wrong with your figure."

As much as she wanted to believe Alex, she knew differently. "In the real world perhaps, but we're talking fashion, where a size six is fat. I'm a size eight." She winced slightly at the lie. She was almost a size ten, but she wasn't ready to say it aloud. She was a "big girl" compared with the other models in the runway shows for Harrington, but the audience always responded well to her when she strutted down the catwalk.

"The Dianne line is still popular."

She placed the glass on the white tablecloth and stared across at him. "How would you know?"

For a moment, she thought he would evade, which was unusual. Alex always spoke his mind. "Catherine keeps up with you, and she keeps me informed."

Dianne didn't know why she felt a small dip of disappointment that he hadn't checked for himself, but what man—besides those directly connected to the industry—checked trends?

"Your food." The server placed the dishes on the table, then left.

Alex bowed his head to bless their food and picked up his fork. Dianne picked up hers as well, but her attention was snagged by the sight and aroma of Alex's food. Her mouth watered. She'd only had water that day. There'd been nothing else edible in the refrigerator. She'd been in Europe for the past three months.

"Hand me your plate."

"What?" Dianne's startled gaze lifted from his food.

Alex reached across the table and picked up her plate. "I'm not going to sit here and let you be hungry."

He placed half of his beef next to her bed of spinach. He speared an asparagus.

"Alex, I can't—"

"You're not starving yourself," he said, adding roasted potatoes to her plate. "When will you see this René again?"

"I'm flying out Tuesday morning after the board meeting," she told him, staring at the plate. Food had always been her weakness. It had comforted her when her life was going wrong, which was more often than not. Yet the thought of leaving Alex troubled her more than facing René.

"There's a fitness center in my apartment building. I'll work out with you in the evenings." He picked up his fork. "You are not starving yourself to please anyone," he repeated.

Again, Dianne tucked her head. Alex was too kind to say it, but the word hung between them. He and Catherine had witnessed her embarrassment and always tried to help. Her mother had put Dianne on a strict diet four times before she graduated from high school, saying she was too fat and an embarrassment.

"You're a beautiful woman," Alex said softly. "If you don't believe me, just look around the restaurant."

Dianne lifted her head. She didn't care what other men thought of her. Something soft unfurled inside her. Alex might be a lawyer, and lawyers often manipulated words and downright lied when it suited them. He might if it was necessary to help her, but he'd never lied to her.

He'd seen her at her lowest points in life and never judged, just went out of his way to help. When her mother put her on her first diet at age ten, he and Catherine made sure she got more than the prescribed thousand calories a day. They got her moving to lose the thirty pounds she'd packed on from overeating and hanging out in front of the TV.

A thought hit. Didn't people burn calories having sex? With that titillating idea in mind, she picked up her fork. "You were merciless about me riding my bike and running."

"I wanted your mother off your case."

They both knew that would never happen permanently. She forked in a bit of beef and roasted potatoes. Moaned. "Why are the good things so bad for you?"

Something crossed his face. Worried, Dianne lowered her fork. "Are you all right?"

"It's nothing." He twisted in his seat, reached for his glass, and gulped his water. "What time are you leaving Tuesday?"

She stared at him a few moments longer, but seeing him pick up his fork and begin to eat, she answered his question. "Not sure. I'm picking up my itinerary Monday morning after I meet the new CEO of Harrington House, Theo Boswell."

Alex's brows lifted. "They're not telling you until then?"

Shrugging, she cut into her asparagus. The combination of foods was delicious. She thought of the pounds she needed to lose then pushed it out of her head. "Things have changed since Grandfather was CEO. The new guy is more hands-on."

Alex placed his fork on his plate. "You need a contract."

Dianne laughed. "You're being a lawyer again."

"Because I've seen too many people get the shaft from going on trust. You have nothing to protect you if the new CEO decides to make drastic changes to the D line and go in a different direction." His eyes narrowed. "Perhaps I should go with you."

"Not necessary." Unworried, Dianne placed her fork on her nearly empty salad plate. "Mom and Dad have a controlling interest in Harrington House. You said yourself, the D line is doing well. My parents enjoy living the life of leisure, and the profits from the company give them that. I'm secure. Don't worry."

He finally smiled. "Force of habit."

She smiled back. "I'm a big girl now."

"A beautiful one."

There it was again, the flirtation. This time his expression didn't change; he kept those beautiful midnight-black eyes of his on her. Dianne felt heat course through her body as she stared at him.

"Anything else? Dessert. Coffee?" the waiter asked.

"Dianne?" Alex asked.

What she wanted wasn't on the menu. "No, thank you."

Alex pulled a business card and pen from the inside of his jacket. "In case you've forgotten, I'll give you my address again. I should be home by six." He handed the thick vellum card to her. "Does that work for you?"

Dianne took the card and barely glanced at it. Alex and Catherine had scary IQs. Dianne had begun modeling after she graduated from high school and had never obtained a college degree. She'd always been a bit intimidated by their intelligence. "I remember where you live. I'm not that much of a bubblehead," she said tightly.

His head came up sharply. "No, you're not. Only an idiot would think you were."

Sighing, Dianne leaned back in her seat. "I overreacted. Sorry."

"Jet lag." Alex signaled for the check. "I'll get you a cab so you can go back to your place, guzzle more water, and rest."

He'd forgiven her, excused her bad manners. She didn't have to think long to remember all the times Alex had taken up for her when her parents had questioned her intelligence or had been ashamed of her—until the D line and she were a success. Then her parents couldn't tell the friends and media enough about how they'd always known she was special, just like her parents.

Dianne waited until he'd paid the check. "Alex, I need to ask you a question."

"Sure."

"I'm invited to a party tonight in the Village. Would you be my date?" His indulgent smile slipped for a fraction of a second. "It should be fun. Come on," she urged.

"What about your exercise?" he asked.

"There'll be dancing," she said, smiling at him. "Please."

"All right," he said, rising to hold her chair. "What time should I pick you up?"

"Nine."

Taking her arm, he led her outside and hailed her a cab. When one pulled up, he opened the door and reminded her, "Rest and water."

She grinned at him. "I will. I want to be ready for tonight. See you at nine."

Closing the door, Alex watched the cab pull away, a smile on his face. He might owe Sin and C. J. a case of their favorite scotch. Maybe, just maybe his feelings weren't one-sided.

It was becoming much too difficult to keep playing the good friend. The problem was, if he was wrong, he was asking for his heart to be handed to him on a platter. But he'd become too used to watching over her. Not even to protect himself could he give up the chance to be with her.

He'd see how the night went and then make a decision. He just hoped he was up to it.

Alex thought he was prepared to walk the increasingly blurry line between friend and a man in love—until Dianne opened her door. His heart plopped at her feet. She was dangerous and tempting in a red, fitted gown that stopped midthigh. His throat dried. Whatever he had been telling himself about his restraint went out the window.

He wanted her with an intensity he'd never felt before. He craved what he couldn't have.

"Hi, Alex. Right on time." Taking his arm, she gently

pulled him inside. "I'll get my clutch and then we can go."

He watched her walk away and wanted to whimper. On closer observation, he saw that the skirt of the gown wrapped and was held with a large bow in back. Any man breathing would want to give the bow a strong tug . . . with his teeth.

She bent, the satin material tightening over her hips. He'd have sent up a prayer if he thought that might help. She came back, stopping mere inches from him. If the dress wasn't enough, her fragrance, a mixture of oranges and jasmine, grabbed him by the throat.

"Alex, are you all right?"

"That's some dress," he managed.

She chuckled, a teasing sound that sent another punch straight below the waist. "It's from the latest D line. Glad you like." She presented him her back, and glanced over her shoulder. "Is the bow straight? I had a hard time."

He swallowed, managed to nod. Her back was gloriously bare.

"You're sure?" she questioned with a wrinkle of her pretty nose. "I don't want to go out not looking right. Appearances are supremely important when you represent the line. You won't hurt my feeling if you have to retie it."

"It's fine," he said, his voice rough. "The car is waiting downstairs."

"Car?" She faced him.

Alex reached for the doorknob in desperation. They had to get out of there before he lost it. "I wasn't sure how long you wanted to stay or about parking."

She looped her arm through his. "You always think of everything."

Alex closed her door, tested the lock, and started for the elevator. If only that were the truth.

Dianne was walking on air by the time they reached Sonya's apartment. Alex was definitely thinking of her more as a woman than as a friend. Good, because the more she was around him, the more she thought of him as the man she wanted to be her first lover. A pang of regret hit as he rang the doorbell of Sonya's apartment. Dianne wished she could keep him as a friend and as a lover, but that would be impossible. He'd eventually get bored with her. She wasn't in his league intellectually.

The door opened and with it come a loud blast of John Mayer singing. J. J. stood frowning at her and blocking the entrance. "Dianne."

"Hello, J. J.," Dianne greeted with a wide smile. J. J., in a black silk shirt and linen pants, was a swimsuit model who lived in the same building. He was also Sonya's sometime lover.

When he continued to stare at her, Dianne stepped forward so he'd have to move back. She'd just have to bluff it through. She'd attended one of Sonya's party's months ago, and that had been enough for Dianne to consider never going again. There had been too much heavy drinking and hard partying. She'd had to threaten to call the police before a man would let her leave. She and Sonya had never been close; after the incident their relationship was strained even more, and everyone knew it.

Dianne just hoped J. J. didn't question her now as to why she was there. "J. J. Louis, meet Alex Stewart. Is Sonya around?"

J. J. finally closed the door, still looking at her with puzzlement. "In this crush someplace."

"We'll find her." Dianne clutched Alex's arm and moved through the throng of people and a haze of smoke. "Sonya is a model as well, but she's freelance. We met years ago in Paris."

"I see," Alex said, his brows bunched.

Dianne forged ahead. She couldn't tell if there was censure in his voice or not. "There she is. Hi, Sonya."

Sonya's green eyes narrowed on Dianne, then moved to Alex and stayed. She actually licked her full red lips. In a skintight black dress that barely covered her hips, the tall brunette air-kissed Dianne's cheeks, then returned her greedy eyes to Alex. "Well, well. Who have we here?"

"Mine," Dianne said, startled by the passion and possessiveness of that one word. She didn't dare look at Alex to see his reaction.

Sonya's gaze flickered over him again. "I don't suppose it would do any good to ask you to share."

"No, it wouldn't," Alex answered, his voice decisive and unbending.

Dianne grinned. "Nice party. J. J. let us in."

Sonya wrinkled her nose. "About time he did something useful. He hasn't had a callback in weeks. He may be on his way out."

Dianne felt a quick stab of pity. Old models, like old actresses, had few options. Alex's arm tightened around her. That wouldn't happen to her. Her parents had controlling interest in the company. Somehow she'd lose the ten pounds before Tuesday.

"He should have expected it. He's thirty, for goodness' sake, and not as toned as he used to be." Sonya smirked as she held a cocktail in one hand and a thin cigarette in the other.

Dianne was thirty-two. Her stomach clenched.

"He's lucky I even tolerated him this long," Sonya continued.

Another reason Dianne had attended only one of Sonya's parties before tonight despite numerous invitations. She was vain and egotistical. She'd step over her grandmother to get where she wanted. "I think we'll circulate."

Sonya shifted so she was closer to Alex. "Please enjoy yourselves and come back anytime. I'm not flying out until after a photo shoot in a couple of weeks."

"Thank you. Safe travel," Alex said, leading Dianne toward the small area they'd set up for the dance floor.

"Sorry about that," Dianne said as he placed his hand on her waist.

"Just answer one question," he said.

She smiled up into his serious face. "Depends on the question."

He glanced around the loud, crowded room, his displeasure obvious. "Why did you want to come here?"

She was on the precipice, but she wanted to be honest with him. "I'm trying to make a decision about something, and you're a part of that decision."

He nodded. "As a lawyer or as a friend?"

She moistened her lips and watched his hot gaze follow. Her skin tingled. "Neither."

"Bud, you ever heard of no parking on the dance floor, especially with a woman this gorgeous?" a tall man in a well-cut suit said. "Let's boogie, baby."

"You ever heard of fools treading where others fear?" Alex asked without missing a beat.

The smile vanished from the man's face. He looked at Alex and decided he didn't want to dance with Dianne after all.

"Then as what?" Alex asked, the man already forgotten.

"Why don't I tell you later," she said, trying to calm her racing heart. Alex could be a possessive warrior. No man was getting near his woman. The thought thrilled her.

He pulled her into his arms, his hand splayed on her bare back. Dianne felt hot, shivery. She wanted to be closer still, to press her lips and her body to his. Her skin felt tight.

Her body reacted so strongly to his. She needed to know if it was just him or her need to be loved and wanted. But she'd felt nothing with Truss, except a need to be with Alex. The song ended. Reluctantly she straightened. She stared up into his eyes, which seemed to be even darker, more piercing. Her heart raced.

"My turn."

"No," Alex bit out, never taking his gaze from her.

"Yes." She needed a moment. Dianne turned blindly toward the man to test her reaction and wanted to groan.

Roscoe Lewis was a shoe designer who thought of himself as a ladies' man. His ego was the size of Alaska. He bedded a lot of his models and bragged about it. He might be handsome, but he was slime.

Roscoe winked at Alex and pulled Dianne into his arms. His smile turned into a frown when she placed her hand on his chest to keep him from drawing her closer. "Hey."

"Hey, back at you," Dianne said, a sweet smile on her face.

"You always thought you were better than the rest of us lesser mortals," he said harshly.

Dianne had heard it before. Since she didn't party and seldom dated, many of those in the fashion industry thought she was stuck up. "I thought you wanted to dance, not discuss my character. Since you don't." She turned to walk away.

"You—" An angry frown on Roscoe's face, he started after her. "Come back here."

Dianne kept walking toward Alex. She didn't like the hard look on his face. She didn't understand until he stepped past her. "I wouldn't touch that sash. Not unless you want a broken hand," Alex said, moving Dianne behind him.

The loud conversation, the clinking of glasses stopped. "Do you know who I am?" Roscoe asked, his eyes harsh.

"Besides scum, no, and I don't care."

Roscoe's head jerked back as if he'd been struck. He bristled. "You'll never work in this industry again."

Dianne laughed. Heads turned to her. "He has the

looks, but he's a lawyer, a darn good one. Believe me, you don't want to mess with him or his well-connected family."

Roscoe sneered. "I have connections as well."

"They don't reach the US Senate and that's just the tip of a very deep iceberg you don't want to run up against." Dianne turned to find Sonya. "Thanks for the invite. We must run." Air-kissing again, Dianne looped her arm through Alex's and left the apartment.

He was as stiff as a board. She glanced at him through her lashes. A muscle leaped in his jaw. She waited until they were in the car before asking, "Are you angry at me or Roscoe?"

"I fight my own battles," he said. "I don't use my family connections."

"I'm sorry." She sighed. She should have known. "I forget that your family and in-laws are different." Her family and a lot of the people she was around tossed influential names about like confetti. "If you won't be mad with me, I promise not to forget again."

The corners of his mouth kicked up. "I never could stay upset with you for long."

She relaxed against the seat. "You've had practice. Ruining the rim on your bike, letting your hamster out, leaving your favorite book of poetry out when it rained. I could go on."

"You were trying to put up my bike when I left it outside. It wasn't your fault I was careless, or that the bike was too heavy for you and it fell," he said, watching her face. "You were trying to feed Charlie. The weatherman forecast sunshine."

She stared at Alex. Was there another man who understood her as well?

"We're here," Alex announced as the car pulled up at the curb of her apartment.

Taking his hand, Dianne got out, nodding to the doorman on duty. Crossing the opulent lobby, they went to the bank of elevators. The apartment was another perk of being "The Face" of the House of Harrington. There was also an apartment in Paris. They were silent on the ride in the elevator and the walk to her door.

Opening her door, she stepped inside. "Please come in."

Alex seemed to hesitate for a moment before entering. He looked around. "Very nice. You've changed things since I was here last."

She wasn't surprised Alex had noticed. "*Cosmo* had a spread on where I live several months ago and Granddad thought the place needed to be redone," she told him. "The company hired a decorator. Luckily, she and I agreed on the changes."

Worry crossed his face. "Is this place in your name on the lease?"

"Don't worry, Alex." She tossed her clutch on the sofa. "Would you like something to drink?"

He took a step closer. "Just the answer to my question. Why did you want me to go to a party that you obviously didn't want to go to?"

"I'm not sure I can explain," she said.

"Try."

She gazed up into his patient eyes. "Perhaps a demonstration would be better." Closing the short distance between them, she circled his neck with her arms and plastered her body and lips against him.

Alex saw her moving toward him, could have stepped back or stopped her, anything to avert what he knew would be his downfall. Or was it his forbidden fantasy come true? At the moment her mouth touched his, he was still thinking. That all changed when the tip of her tongue slid inside his mouth.

His body went on full, greedy alert. Hands that hadn't known what to do reached for her, pulling her even closer, deepening the kiss. The taste of her was rich, exotic, just like the perfume that had grabbed him by the throat two seconds after he'd seen her. With her lush breasts pressed against him, her incredible body flush against him, he ceased to think. His hands and mouth took over while his brain took a vacation.

She was soft—everywhere. The slim back, the slender arms. His hand cupped her hips to bring her incredible softness closer still. She moved seductively against his rigid hardness. The top of his head almost exploded.

This woman, Dianne, was all that he had ever wanted, desired, and she wanted him, too. He stilled as the brain on vacation decided to return. He tried his best to push the thought *Why now* away, but his brain was having none of it. He'd always been inquisitive and sought logical answers. Dianne kissing him like she wanted to crawl into him wasn't logical.

Lifting his head, he broke the kiss, stared down into her face flushed with desire, watched her eyes full of unquenched need. He cursed his brain and locked his arms to keep from lowering his head and damning the reason she had finally seen him as a man and not as the brother of her best friend.

"Why?"

"W-what?" she murmured, still looking a bit dazed.

Alex struggled not to be peacock-proud that he'd put that look on her face. Answers. "Why me? Why now? Why the party?"

Her head lowered until her forehead rested on his chest. "Your heart is beating fast."

"Dianne," he said tightly. He might go to the mat for her, but she also knew he liked straight answers.

Her head lifted. Desire still shimmered in her incredible light brown eyes, but there was also something else there.

Vulnerability.

He started to pull her back into his arms, but she pushed away. Standing there with her back to him, she looked alone. She'd had few people in her life who really loved her.

"Dianne," he said, softly, reaching out to lightly touch her shoulder. At least that was what he'd intended, but it turned into a caress. His hand clenched. He wondered if they could ever go back to before the kiss.

She turned and stared at him. The look direct. There was nothing vulnerable about her now. "I thought it would be kind of obvious what I want from you."

His body hardened. *Down boy.* "Perhaps you should tell me so there are no mistakes."

"Sounds like a lawyer." She smiled, tilted her head flirtatiously, then threaded her fingers through the lustrous mane of long black hair that he'd dreamed of seeing on his pillow, stroking his chest. "Alexander McCall Stewart, I want you to be my first lover. Is that plain enough?"

Chapter 5

Alex was stunned. He simply stared at Dianne.

He wasn't stupid enough to think the kiss or the straight-on request had been teasing. Dianne wasn't the teasing or impulsive type.

He was still hung up on *first*. He stared at the beautiful and desirable woman before him and couldn't reconcile this with the fact that she hadn't been intimate with anyone before. "You haven't—" He couldn't go on. There were too many nights that he'd tortured himself with thoughts that she was in bed with another man.

She gazed up at him through a sweep of long black lashes. "Mrs. Stewart and Catherine's doing."

"Mother and Catherine?"

Sighing, she waved him to a side chair in the great room, then took a seat on the mile-long white sofa. She'd barely settled before she picked up a blue silk throw pillow, hugged it to her stomach, and wrapped her arms around it. "When your mother was giving talks to Catherine about the birds and the bees, and the hormonal, sex-driven cravings of young boys, she included me." Dianne shrugged. "Guess she knew my parents weren't going to do it. Early on Catherine decided to wait to be intimate until she was married, and since I loved her and wanted to be like her, I decided to wait, too."

Her eyes narrowed. "Then that no-good jerk broke off their engagement because Catherine found out after her operation that she couldn't have children. I wanted to knock his head into a brick wall," she finished angrily.

Alex's eyes fired. "I went looking for him, but the cowardly bastard had left town. Dad made me see that putting him in the hospital wouldn't help Catherine get over the pain of his desertion." He rubbed his fists. "It sure would have made *me* feel better."

"She's happier with Luke."

"And that's the only reason I didn't beat him to a slimy pulp when I ran into him in Boston a couple of months ago when I went there on business." Alex settled back in his wing chair. "What changed your mind about waiting?"

She cut him a look. "Redirecting the witness, counselor?"

He leaned forward. He had to know. "Yes."

Dianne bit her lower lip, picked at the fringe tassel on the pillow. "Don't you think it's time?"

"What do you think?"

Her eyes lanced up to him; the pillow followed. He caught it, then tossed it on the chair next to him. "Your body. Your decision."

Dianne blew out a breath, then leaned her head back against the sofa. "You've always understood me better than anyone, even Catherine. I'm hoping you'll understand this time as well."

"I'm listening." And jumping for joy on the inside.

She came upright, wrapped her slim arms around her waist, and paced. "You already know what I'm about to say although we've never discussed it out loud." She stopped and looked at him. "My parents use me when convenient and forget about me the rest of the time. My maternal grandparents died when I was small. My daddy's parents were seldom in my life since they lived in New York and we lived in Boston."

She swallowed. "Once my paternal grandmother died, I went to live with Grandfather because my parents thought if I did, they wouldn't have to be worried with an awkward, overweight, unwanted disappointment of a daughter."

Alex shot to his feet. "Don't."

She held up her hand. "Please. I'm not feeling too sorry for myself. There's a point to this."

He took his seat.

She sent him a wan smile. "I was Granddad's hope for the House of Harrington to continue. Dad had no interest in the firm except the monthly deposit to his checking account. I worked hard, but I couldn't create from nothing. I could see how to enhance, but my grandfather didn't think any of my designs were marketable." She smiled, this time for real.

"He was so conscious of hurting my feelings, so patient, so supportive. A lot like you and your family. When I suggested a line for women my age, and ideas, he was over the moon."

"So you did have what it took to design, and now you're famous."

"And alone." She folded her arms. "I took you to the party because I wasn't sure about asking you to be the one. I wanted to see if the little zaps that happened to us at Sabra's party were an accident, see if you were attracted to me."

"What did you decide?" he asked with more calm than he felt. He burned for her. Her parents were selfish idiots.

"They weren't accidents, but I forgot an important part of my decision." Her face softened and her arms dropped to her sides. "At Sabra's party, I saw something else. Unconditional love. The couples there had that in abundance. They'd go the ends of the world for each other. I want that before I die—if only for a little while."

He'd love her for a lifetime and beyond if she let him. He came to his feet and started toward her. "I accept with pleasure."

She swallowed. Both hands came up this time. He kept walking. Her trembling hands flexed on the fine wool of his suit jacket. "I guess it's sort of late, but are you seeing anyone, or do you have a girlfriend?"

"No girlfriend and not seeing anyone," he answered. "I wouldn't have kissed you if I were."

"Somehow I knew that, but I had to ask," she said softly.

"Understandable. Any other questions or concerns?"

"I just want you to know that I don't expect it to last." He frowned and she rushed on. "Ground rules first. One, we stay friends afterward. I won't risk that for an affair. You're too important to me."

Easy. He had no intention of letting her go. "Agreed."

"Rule two. You don't pretend." Her voice shook, then firmed. "I want to know how it feels when a man looks at me as if I'm his world. I've been told too many lies or ignored in the past. If you don't feel it, please don't fake it."

Easy again. "Agreed." His hands settled at her waist. He stared into her uncertain, wistful eyes. Love. She wanted love when that was all he'd ever wanted to give her. His lips brushed against hers. Her breath hitched. Her hands clenched. "I could kiss you forever."

Sighing, she leaned into him. "No one has ever made me feel this—this edgy way—when he kissed me before."

His hand tightened. Her eyes widened.

"What?"

"Rule. I don't want to hear about you kissing or anything else with another man," he said, aware of how Neanderthal and unfair he sounded.

A slow smile curved her beautifully shaped mouth upward. "You're jealous."

"I'm glad I can entertain you."

Her arms went around his neck. "Alex," she breathed, and her voice hitched. "No one has ever cared enough to be jealous." She leaned back. "I'm glad it's you."

He kissed her. He couldn't help it. She was so lovable and thought she wasn't. His tongue swept inside her mouth, tasting the sweetness. "I'm glad you chose me, too. I care about you. If I didn't, I would have never agreed."

"Do . . . do we do it now?" she asked with a mixture of uncertainly and excitement. "I put candles and fresh flowers in the bedroom in case you said yes."

He kissed her trembling palm. "We'll save them for another time. How about we get to know each other again, date and have fun first."

"It's Tuesday. I leave in a week." She pulled her lower lip between her teeth.

"Some things shouldn't be rushed." He wanted her to know when they made love that it wasn't an obligation, but a pleasure.

"All right. You're the experienced one in this," she said.

He found he didn't want to think of the other women before Dianne. He started to enact another rule, then changed his mind. There might have been women before Dianne, but she would be the last. "People falling in love can't wait to see each other. So how about breakfast in the morning?"

The quick smile faded. She tucked her head.

"What?" His finger lifted her chin. "Tell me. They also talk and are honest with each other."

She looked at him as if she knew he lied and remained silent.

"Do you think if Catherine had a problem, Luke wouldn't move heaven and earth to solve it?" he asked. "The ones who make it work are honest and talk things out."

"The weight thing," she whispered.

If that René guy ever showed up in New York, Alex was going to have a strong talk with him. "Many restaurants have light or low-cal menus. What time is good for me to pick you up?"

"Whenever," she told him. "For the first time I'm not scheduled for any interviews or fittings. My time is my own. You, on the other hand, are always booked for weeks."

"You're usually all over the place when you're here," he said.

"I know. I mentioned that to the PR rep at Harrington in New York and she said they wanted to give me a chance to relax after the last fashion show," she told him. "It seems we have perfect timing."

Alex wasn't so sure, but he let it slide. "Is eight all right? I'm usually at the office by nine."

"Fine. Despite what you might have heard about the lazy life of models, we work hard and often get up pretty early for morning shoots or to start preparing for a fashion show," she said. "I'll be ready."

"Good." He kissed her, then went to the door. "Good night, beautiful."

"Good night, Alex." On impulse, she lifted on tiptoes to brush her lips against his. His arm curved around her waist, dragging her to him. His mouth ravished hers, then she was free.

Dianne opened her eyes to see him striding down the hall. He stepped in the elevator and turned. Even from this distance, she felt the burning desire in his eyes. He wanted her. The doors closed.

Stepping back into her apartment, Dianne shut and locked the door. The building had twenty-four-hour security and a doorman, but her grandfather had taught her to always use the extra lock because she traveled so much.

Dianne started for her bedroom, but her shaky legs had other ideas. She plopped down in the same chair Alex had vacated.

We're going to be lovers.

Knowing it was really going to happen was vastly different from just thinking about it. Pushing up from the chair, glad her legs supported her, she went to her bedroom, untying the sash as she went. In front of the ten-by-four-foot mirror, she tossed the dress on the bed. In a red demi-bra and thong, she tried to study her body impartially.

Nothing jiggled except her breasts. She couldn't pinch an inch at her waist. But René thought she needed to lose ten pounds.

He's an idiot.

Dianne chuckled on remembering Alex's incensed words and firmly turned away from the mirror. Alex thought she was beautiful. Tonight, that was enough.

Alex was pensive on the car ride to his apartment. Dianne wanted a no-strings affair; he wanted a lifetime. How to get her from what she thought she wanted to where he wanted them to end up was the big question. After paying the driver, he got out, spoke to the doorman, and went to the elevator. Inside, he punched his floor.

The chrome-and-glass enclosure climbed swiftly to his destination. Getting off, he went to his apartment. Sin lived one floor up; C. J., one floor down. Inside, Alex went straight to his bedroom and undressed. He thought better in the shower.

Moments later he stepped naked beneath the sixteen jet streams. Dianne needed to be courted and loved. She needed to know that she was smart and worthwhile. It made him mad as hell that she didn't think she was. It scared him spitless that she might have gone to some other man. He shook the disturbing thought away.

She hadn't. He dealt in facts. He just had to remember that.

The hard fact was that in the coming days he had to bind her to him with love, with sex if he had to. When Tuesday came, she wasn't walking out of his life again. She *was* his life. But she wasn't ready to hear that.

She wanted them to be lovers and friends, with emphasis on friends. She didn't expect the relationship to last. Her parents hadn't been there for her so she didn't think anyone else would be. He was going to show her how wrong she was.

Shutting off the water, he stepped out of the open travertine enclosure and reached for the fluffy white towel on the heated rack. He'd been handed his dream; now all he had to do was make sure he kept it.

It stood to reason that Dianne wanted and deserved the whole courtship package. She wanted to feel as special as she was. He'd give her memories to last two lifetimes.

In his bedroom, he picked up the phone and dialed. "Radcliffe's, where our priority is your dining pleasure."

"Ms. Radcliffe, please. Alex Stewart calling."

"Certainly, Mr. Stewart. Please hold."

Gladly, he thought.

"Talk quickly, Alex, the restaurant is packed," Summer Radcliffe told him.

He could just imagine. Radcliffe's was one of the hottest restaurants in the city. Four years ago Summer had taken the city by storm with the elegant upscale restaurant, which now had a two-month waiting list. "Any chance I can get reservations for tomorrow night? It's important."

"Don't tell me a woman has finally captured the attention of one of the renegades."

He shifted on the bed. They teased one another, but they didn't like other people referring to them as the renegades. "You know we're sensitive about that name."

"I noticed you didn't deny the woman is more than a casual date," she said.

"I didn't say it was a woman," he countered.

Summer laughed, a husky, sultry sound that had captured the attention of more than one man when he was with her. She attracted men like a magnet. "But it is, isn't it? I already know your sister and your other relatives left yesterday."

"All right, it's a woman. About the reservations?"

"Since I'm dying to see her, be here at nine."

"Thanks, Summer, and I know you have flowers on the table, but is it all right if I send over a special bouquet for the table?"

"Now I'm really anxious to see her. Maybe Sin and C. J. will take notice."

"Your cousin C. J. likes women, but he's a confirmed bachelor who likes his man-cave bar too much to settle down. Sin is just as footloose with his consulting firm," Alex said, reminding Summer of what she already knew. "They play hard, but they work harder."

"You still have their backs," Summer snorted.

"Just like they have mine," Alex said, thinking of their backing him to go after Dianne.

"See you tomorrow. Bye."

"Bye." Alex hung up and smiled. "Now it begins."

Dianne was ready when Alex picked her up at eight. Barely. She had three walk-in closets full of the latest summer D designs, plus several outfits that she'd kept from previous seasons, but she'd had a difficult time finding the right thing to wear.

Sure, she'd had dates before, interviews, but none had left her so nervous. She laughed with the sheer pleasure of having the opportunity.

"Hi," she said, greeting him in an ivory sand-washed silk oversized safari shirt, slim jeans, and wedge heels.

"Hi," Alex greeted, his gaze running appreciatively over her. "Ready for breakfast?"

"For breakfast and whatever you have planned," she said boldly. There was no sense being coy. She wanted it all, and that's what she was going to get.

For an answer, he pulled her into his arms, kissing her. "That for starters."

Her breath trembled over her lips. "Well, I like how you think."

"Come on." Taking her hand, he led her from the apartment.

Laughing, Dianne eagerly went with him, enjoying

just being with Alex, marveling that it was different somehow—or perhaps she was different. The restaurant was a short two blocks away. They were lucky enough to grab a table by the window. She picked up the menu and almost sighed on seeing a picture of waffles covered with strawberries, whipped cream, and pecans.

"You decide yet?" Alex asked.

"Unfortunately," Dianne said. "Egg white. Tonic water."

"What are you having?" the waitress asked, her pencil poised over a narrow pad.

"Two egg whites and tonic water," Alex ordered, giving the waitress his menu.

"You don't have to have that because I am," she protested.

Alex plucked the menu from her hand. "It's probably for the best. We have reservations at Radcliffe's tonight and there's not a low-cal dish on the menu."

She'd heard of the five-star restaurant, but never been there. She braced her folded arms on the table. "The wait time to get reservations is even greater at Radcliffe's than Le Cirque. Give."

"Your tonic water?" the server said, then left.

Alex picked up his glass. "The owner, Summer Radcliffe, is a friend as well as a client of mine, and the cousin of one of my best friends, C. J. Callahan."

"I've never stayed in one place long enough to have friends, real friends," she said a bit wistfully.

"You could always scale back a bit, perhaps stay in New York and design again," he said casually.

Dianne didn't like the sickening fear she felt and

tried not to show it. Modeling was all she knew. "It's not so bad, and I haven't designed anything in years."

"Your food."

Dianne was glad for the interruption until she looked down at her plate, then up at Alex. "What time are you picking me up for dinner tonight?"

Alex laughed and picked up his fork. "Maybe it tastes better than it looks." He took a bite, grimaced, and pushed away his plate. "Eight-thirty. We'll order appetizers the moment we're seated."

Dianne grinned back at him. "As I said, I like how think, counselor."

"I'm counting on it."

Alex was nervous and excited as their cab pulled up in front of Radcliffe's. Those without reservations were already forming a line outside the restaurant in the hope someone canceled or missed their reservations. He'd owe Summer for this, but she'd probably bean him if he did any more than say thanks.

He paid the driver, then helped Dianne out of the cab. He'd chosen Radcliffe's for a number of reasons, one being that he wanted their first official date to be a place they would look back on later with happiness. He also wanted Dianne to have a great time, feel as special as she was, meet his friends, and let them become hers. She needed friends. He planned to see that she had the opportunity.

"Come on." With his arm around her waist, he ushered her under the red awning into the opulent restaurant. Dark paneled walls abounded. The original oil paintings and crystal sconces gave the room an old-world charm. A smiling hostess in a beautiful yellow silk dress greeted them.

"Good evening, Mr. Stewart. Miss. Your table is ready. Please follow me." Plucking two menus, she threaded her way through the tables. She stopped near the back by a walled fish tank with blue and yellow tropical fish and coral. She reached for Dianne's chair.

"Thanks. I'll get it." Alex pulled out Dianne's red brocade-upholstered chair, then took his seat and accepted a menu.

"Do you require the sommelier or can I have the pleasure of putting in your drink order?" she asked.

Dianne smiled across the table at Alex. "White wine since I've been a good girl."

Alex grinned back. "Make that two, and crab cakes. We're sort of hungry."

The woman smiled. "I'll send your drinks right over and put in your order. Perry, your waiter, will be here shortly." The young woman moved away.

Dianne looked at Alex, then around the room. "This place is fabulous. I can see why the long wait."

"The food is just as good," Alex said. "Summer's parents were in the restaurant business, and she learned from them."

"Your drinks." The server placed the glasses on the table, then left.

"Are they retired?" Dianne asked, reaching for her glass.

Sadness touched Alex's face. "They were both killed in an automobile accident when she was eighteen."

"How tragic for her." Dianne pulled her hand back and glanced around again. "From what I can see, her parents would be proud."

"I think they would be as well," said a sultry voice.

Alex came to his feet. Summer looked as exotically beautiful as usual with her caramel skin, doe-shaped eyes, and curly black hair that reached to the middle of her slim back. "Dianne Harrington. Summer Radcliffe, owner of Radcliffe's."

Dianne warmly extended her hand. "Hi. I've heard nothing but praise about your restaurant. I can't wait to taste the food. Alex says it's great."

"Thank you. We strive for nothing less than the best for our customers." Summer smiled at Alex. "Waiting paid off for you."

His grin widened. "Don't I know it."

"Enjoy Radcliffe's. If there is anything I or my staff can do to make your dining experience more pleasurable, please let us know," Summer said, then moved away.

"She's very nice." Dianne leaned over the table as Alex retook his seat. "I could kiss you for not going all gaga over her. She's gorgeous."

Alex frowned. "I've never thought of Summer romantically. She's just C. J.'s cousin."

Dianne eased out of her seat, kissed Alex on the cheek, then returned to the chair. "You're something, counselor."

"Good evening, I'm your waiter, Perry. Your crab cakes." He placed the white platter on the table. "Are you ready to order?"

Smiling apologetically, Dianne opened her menu. "Not yet. Sorry."

"Please give us a few minutes," Alex said to the waiter.

"I can't decide," Dianne said, studying her menu.

"Order some of everything or we could share," Alex suggested. "I'm thinking a Radcliffe's Greek salad, the steak and lobster. What caught your eye?"

"Besides you?" She peeked over the menu and grinned at him.

He smiled back. "You already have me." Her eyes softened. It was liberating not to have to watch what he said to her. "The menu," he reminded her.

Dianne looked at the oversized, leather-bound menu. "Field green salad and the salmon."

Alex stared at her. "Remember, no dieting."

She laughed, a soft sound that made his heart sing. "I love salmon."

"Salmon it is." One day, if he were blessed and lucky, she'd say she loved him. He signaled the waiter and placed their order.

Dianne handed the waiter the menu and reached for her glass of wine. Her hand paused as she looked at the lush white roses mixed with gardenias in a square crystal vase. She glanced at the nearest table and the one next to it. Both had white lilies in a lotus blossom vase. Dianne's gaze went to Alex, then the arrangement on the table.

"You—you remembered after all these years," she whispered, touching a lush white gardenia petal.

"They used to be your favorite flowers," he said. "You

always said when you grew up you'd have them in your house every day."

"I did for a while, but I was on the go so much I didn't get to enjoy them." She smiled tenderly at him. "Thank you for remembering."

"I've forgotten few things about you."

Dianne got the warm feeling again. She reached her hand out. He caught it.

"Your salads."

Releasing her hand, he bowed his head and blessed their food, then asked, "Have you ever played pool?"

Her eyes lit up with interest. "No."

"We have a monthly pool competition at Callahan's, C. J.'s bar," he explained. "It's this Friday night. I'd like for us to go."

She picked up her fork. "Will you teach me?"

He leaned over and grinned. "It will be my pleasure."

She could already tell it would be her pleasure as well. She took a bite of crab cake, chewed, and swallowed. "This is good. You know, I'm made some bad decisions in my life. Looks like I hit one out of the park this time."

Chapter 6

Dianne's heart was beating a mile a minute as she stopped at her front door. Alex said they'd take it slow, but maybe he'd changed his mind. They'd had a great time at Radcliffe's. She pulled her key from her purse.

"Let me get that."

"Thank you." Dianne's voice sounded shaky, a bit breathless.

After opening the door, Alex handed her the key. She realized he wasn't going to rush her or assume. A bit of her anxiety eased. "Please come in."

He smiled and stepped past her. Closing the door, she continued to the great room, tossing her clutch on the sofa. "What's so funny?" she asked, turning to him.

His hands settled on her waist, and he pulled her closer. Her heart went crazy. Her hands automatically settled on his chest. "You're such a delight."

She blinked. Of all the things she expected him to say, that had never occurred to her. "I am?"

"You are." He brushed his lips tenderly across hers as if he couldn't wait any longer. "I have something to confess."

Since he was looking at her as if he never wanted to let her go, she didn't think she should be worried. "Yes?"

"I've wanted you for a long time."

Surprise widened her eyes and made her knees shake. "You—you have?"

"I didn't say anything because I didn't think I stood a chance, and I didn't want to jeopardize our friendship," he told her.

His thoughts had been so much like hers.

"I just thought you should know up front that, if I didn't care about you, I wouldn't be here." He pulled her closer still, his arms locked around her. "I've dreamed of you in my bed, your hair on my pillow."

Air became harder to draw in. Heat zipped though her veins.

"I want you in all the ways a man can want a woman and then some." His mouth took her, branding her as his. The heat, the pleasure enveloped her. Her hands clutched his shirt and just held on as his mouth and hands ravaged her.

His hands cupped her hips, bringing her more fully against the rigid hardness of his desire. She moaned and pressed closer. Her body felt on fire. She wanted to touch his bare skin, wanted him to touch hers. She pulled up his shirt, ran her hands over the corded muscles of his stomach, his chest, and felt him flinch.

Immediately she jerked her hands and body away. "Sorry. Did I hurt you?"

His eyes blazed. "Only when you're not in my arms."

She took one step back to him, he took the other.

This time she didn't hesitate to touch, to taste, and neither did he.

She was burning in his arms. He couldn't get enough of her. She was so warm, so responsive. He wanted more. Picking her up, he placed her on the sofa, following her down. His body pressed against hers was heaven on earth.

More than his next breath he wanted to slide the side zipper on her little black dress down, pull the dress over her head, and feast on her. If he did, he wouldn't stop. Closing his eyes, he sat up with her in his lap, her head tucked beneath his chin, their breathing off kilter.

"You are a treasure I never allowed myself to believe I'd have," he murmured.

"Alex."

She said his name with such need and reverence, he almost pulled her back down on the sofa. "Taking this slow might be a bit harder than I'd imagined."

"Don't stop on my account," she said.

Hearing the teasing in her voice, he laughed, hugging her to him. "You're something."

Sitting up, she smiled at him. Her finger brushed across his lower lip. "I was just thinking the same thing about you."

He nipped her finger, kissed her on the lips. "I have a conference call in the morning at eight and court at ten or I'd take you to breakfast and lunch where we'd eat real food. What are you doing tomorrow?"

She made a face. "Going to the spa for a body wrap."

"I could do that for you."

She burst out laughing, then leaned against him. "You

can't imagine how wonderful it is not to have to watch what I say to you. You don't mind that I have to lose a few pounds."

"You're perfect."

If only. "Just hearing you say that helps."

The frown on his face didn't clear. "Who are you going to believe? Some jerk or me?"

Because she realized he'd never understand, because he was angry on her behalf, she palmed his face. "You. Always."

He kissed her long and hot and slow. She forgot about her weight and just enjoyed.

The next morning, humming softly to herself, Dianne checked her makeup in the bathroom mirror, then went to her bedroom for her handbag. She was halfway out of the door when she remembered to check the money in her wallet. She'd learned through the years to always keep extra cash in her billfold. That hadn't been possible lately.

Her lips pressed together in annoyance. Ninety-three dollars. Last month's paycheck had been a week late getting to her bank. This time it was ten days and counting. She'd checked her bank account online and it had less than two hundred dollars.

She bit her lower lip. Her clothes might be free, but she had to purchase the undergarments, the designer handbags, shoes, and accessories that went with them. She frowned at the wallet in her hand. She'd had it for two years but it cost almost a thousand dollars, the matching handbag four times that amount. The leopard-print slides on her feet were on sale at five hundred dollars. The eighteen-karat earrings and gold chain around her neck another three thousand.

She picked up the phone on the bed chest and dialed Harrington's New York headquarters. The phone was answered on the second ring.

"House of Harrington."

"Dianne Harrington. Please connect me with Mr. Boswell."

"Yes, Ms. Harrington."

Dianne tossed her wallet toward her handbag. She needed her money. The new CEO was behind this. She just knew it.

There'd been no problems with her paycheck until his appointment. When she'd asked the head of payroll, she'd been directed to his office. His secretary had said it was a payroll error. Not likely since it had never happened before. Her check was in her bank in less than twenty-four hours after the phone call. He clearly wanted her to know he was in charge.

"Ms. Harrington, this is Mr. Boswell's secretary, Ms. Hill. He's in a meeting. How can I help you?"

Dianne had heard the same story twice before from his secretary. "My paycheck hasn't been deposited in my account. Again."

"I'm sorry for the inconvenience," Ms. Hill said. "I can only imagine how annoying this must be. That's why Mr. Boswell is in a meeting, bringing the staff up to par."

"When my grandfather was running the company, it was up to par," Dianne said. There had already been changes and firings in the Paris office. Dianne imagined the same thing was happening in New York.

"I've heard your grandfather was a great man. I believe, given the opportunity, you'll come to feel the same way about Mr. Boswell," Ms. Hill said.

Dianne doubted it. "When can I expect my paycheck?"

"I'll check on it, but if for any unforeseen reason it doesn't show up in your account, I'll have payroll cut you another check while you're in the meeting Monday. Will that work for you?"

"I want it waiting for me when I arrive," Dianne said emphatically.

"Mr. Boswell wants you to have everything that is coming to you. Trust me."

When someone said *Trust me,* her grandfather had told her to watch out. "If I don't have my paycheck by the time I leave the meeting, I'm contacting my lawyer." Alex would get her check and crack some heads in the process—if she told him. She wouldn't. Not now. If she did, he'd get angry on her behalf and then remind her that he'd always said she needed a contract. "Good-bye."

"Good-bye, Ms. Harrington."

Dianne picked up her wallet and put it in her purse. She still had a credit card. She pushed away the worrisome little voice reminding her that it was the company's credit card, and the only one she had.

The nagging little voice didn't stop until the charges for her wrap, pedicure, and manicure—which she added—went through. Tipping her technicians, she left the spa.

She shouldn't have worried, but lately she'd been restless, uneasy. She'd attributed it at first to the loss of her grandfather, but she wasn't so sure anymore. As Sonya had pointed out, thirty was old in the modeling business—at least for some models.

No matter how she tried to push it out of her mind, she worried that she wasn't going to be one of those lucky people who were ageless in the industry. And if she wasn't, she didn't want to think about what would happen to her. Pushing the unsettling thought away, she went window-shopping, a favorite pastime and a business necessity to see what other designers were doing.

Slightly winded, she didn't arrive back at her apartment until a little after four. She'd walked the last ten blocks instead of taking a cab. Despite what Alex said, she had to at least lose a pound or two before she returned to Paris.

She was on her way to the kitchen for a bottle of water when her cell phone rang. Seeing Alex's name, she smiled. "Hi."

"Hi. You have fun at the spa?"

"Yes." She plopped on the sofa, drawing her feet under her. "I thought you were going to be in court."

"I was, but it ended sooner than I expected."

"You must have won. I can hear it in your voice," she mused.

"Yeah," he said. "The insurance company will have to pay the family the money due them."

"It sounds like one of the pro-bono cases you take and never collect the fee, or donate it to charities," she said.

"Sometimes people need help. If I can give it to them, why not?"

Dianne leaned back on the sofa. He was such a great guy. "Congratulations. We'll have to celebrate."

"I'm way ahead of you. I should be there in fifteen minutes. We're going to Central Park. Maybe take a canoe ride. Just relax."

"I'd love that." She came to her feet, snagging her handbag on the way to the bedroom. "I haven't been there in years."

"Neither have I. See you in a bit. Bye."

"Bye."

With his shirtsleeves rolled up almost to his elbows, Alex strolled hand in hand with Dianne though Central Park. He had few free afternoons. He really didn't have one now. He should be going over a brief, but he'd wanted to see Dianne, be with her as much as possible. He wouldn't give anything less than his best for his client, but neither was he willing to forgo the precious time he had left with her.

"This is wonderful," she mused, leaning against him.

He kissed the top of her head. He couldn't agree more. She looked sensational in a sleeveless white sundress that stopped just above her incredible knees. The grass was green, the sky an awesome blue. It was a beautiful day to be with the woman he loved. It felt good just being with her. He tried not to think about her leaving in five days, but the thought kept creeping back into his mind no matter how much he tried to keep it out.

"Although you shouldn't have tempted me earlier,"

Dianne said, a pout on her beautiful face. "You know how weak I am."

Alex stopped, pulled her into his arms, and kissed her for the sheer pleasure it gave him, tasting the mustard from the hot dog she'd just eaten. "Just helping an independent businessman and getting the full Central Park experience."

Dianne, her hands on his chest, smiled up at him. "It was delicious, but I shouldn't have."

"We'll walk it off, or you can help me row the canoe. Come on." He took her hand and they started down the walk again. A couple of women jogged past them. On the grass, people were reading, sleeping, playing Frisbee.

"Oh, Alex. Look."

Hearing the softness in her voice, he followed the direction of her gaze and saw a wedding being performed. The woman wore a long white gown and the man a tuxedo. A small group of people stood around them.

"I hope they'll always be as happy as they are today and have enough love for their children," Dianne said quietly.

He knew she was thinking about her parents. They probably loved each other in their own way, but there was never enough love to include their daughter. "For some, the love only becomes stronger. Children are an extension of that love."

She looked up at him. He saw the doubt and the sadness in her eyes.

"Watch out, man!"

Alex's head came up, around, searching for danger.

Reflexively he pushed Dianne behind him with one hand and caught the Frisbee that would have hit her in the face with the other. He whirled around to her. "Are you all right?"

She smiled up at him. "With you, always."

"Sorry, man. Your woman all right? It got away from me."

"Yes, I'm fine." Dianne curved her arm around Alex's waist.

Alex glanced around and saw a man in his early twenties wearing a sweat-stained Columbia University gray T-shirt. "I can see that."

Alex gave the grinning young man back the Frisbee. "Be more careful in the future."

"Sure thing." With a wave of the Frisbee, he was gone.

"You have great reflexes," she teased.

"Hmmm. I suppose." His arm was around her waist as he stared at the group of men playing.

"What?" Dianne asked, moving in front of him.

He stared down at her. She was beautiful, vibrant. Men desired her. "You're leaving and men will want you."

She palmed his face. "But I won't want them. I never did. You're the only one who makes my heart race, my skin shiver. And I'm here now."

He grabbed her to him and just held on. "I always want to be that man." He kissed her long and deep, wishing it never had to end between then, knowing it would. "After the canoe ride, how about an early movie and then dinner?"

"I have a better idea." She looped her arms around his

neck. "Why don't we rent a movie, watch it at your place, and do our own version of a body wrap," she asked.

Man, how he loved this woman! "I like your idea even better."

Dianne intentionally chose a romantic comedy for them to watch. She wanted to laugh and be happy, and forget the happy couple in the park, forget that for some love didn't last. Yet the closer the couple in the movie came to finally admitting their love for each other, the sadder Dianne became.

For her, there would be no happily-ever-after. She should have realized that she'd want more than a brief affair.

"You're not crying, are you?" Alex teased.

She felt a lump in her throat, but it wasn't for the couple. Sitting beside him on the sofa in his apartment, she kept her head on his chest. "It's allowed."

"He's going to realize he needs her in his life more than his oddball buddies, and she's going to realize that her girlfriends were all wrong about him being all wrong for her."

"I thought you hadn't seen this before," she said.

"It's the only obvious conclusion," Alex said. "Neither of them wants to admit their feelings for the other for fear of being the first and being vulnerable. Caring for someone puts you at risk."

She sat up and stared at him. "That never stopped you," she said with absolute certainty. Alex cared, and he showed it in every possible way.

"Some things are worth the risk."

So simple and so true. She might not ever have it all, but with Alex she'd come very close. She was going to enjoy this time and stop thinking about what couldn't be.

Sitting up, she straddled him, her knees sinking into the sofa cushion beside his hips, her arms around his neck. "Why didn't I ever see this other side of you?"

His hands bracketed her waist. "You've always been busy."

That could be the reason, or it could be that she hadn't thought about "Alex the lover" instead of "Alex the man she could always count on" until she needed one. She leaned her forehead against his. "And selfish."

"We're all selfish."

Her head lifted. "You're doing it again. Defending me."

"If I wasn't selfish, I would have tried to talk you out of us becoming lovers," he told her. "I didn't because I want you too much to be noble. See? Selfish."

She felt the proof of his desire nudging her, yet he calmly held her. "A selfish man would have taken what he wanted that first night. He wouldn't have cared about my feelings or wanted to make this romantic and fun."

His eyes darkened. "I never want you to regret our being together."

"Never. And just so you know." She felt the heat and the hardness of his body. Her lips touched his, gently, then with growing hunger and need. His hands swept up and down her back before settling on her hips, bringing her woman's softness against his growing erection.

Her body shuddered. She wanted more. As if recognizing her feelings, he deepened the kiss, his tongue thrusting deep, tasting and teasing her. Sensations racked her body. Her breasts felt tight. She wanted her hands on him, his on her.

She jerked up the T-shirt he'd changed into when they arrived at his place. His skin was warm, resilient, muscular. The more she felt, the more she wanted to touch him. She was almost light-headed with the need.

"Dianne." He whispered her name in a guttural sound moments before he leaned her backward and fastened his mouth on her aching nipple.

She moaned. Whimpered. Even through the thin cotton-and-lace bra, she felt the suckling deep in the core of her body. The ache intensified. She pressed against him, trying to appease the growing need building between her thighs.

Abruptly he tore his mouth away and pulled her to him. She felt him trembling, felt her own body doing the same.

"I want you so badly."

She wanted him the same desperate way. "I—I never knew."

He leaned her away from him. His eyes were dark with desire. "When we make love, I'm not going to want to let you out of my arms or bed for a long, long time. If I didn't have important court cases tomorrow you wouldn't be leaving tonight, but I won't deny myself this."

The last words were barely out of his mouth before his mouth was on her again, kissing her with passion and long-suppressed hunger. Her arms tightened around his neck. Their mouths clung as if each were starved for the other. She felt wanted, desired.

He devoured her mouth while his hands freely pleasured her body. Much too soon he lifted his head and sat her on the seat beside him, blew out a breath. "You get to me."

It occurred to her that Alex was putting his feelings out there, being vulnerable. It wasn't just sex. She realized she could do no less. She caught his hand and waited until he turned to her. "You kiss me and I forget everything."

"Soon we won't stop at kissing." He stood and picked up the remote control. "The movie credits are rolling. You want to roll the movie back or go for a walk?"

She came to her feet. "Walking might get our minds off other things."

"Or at least keep us from acting on them." Smiling, he reached for her hand. "Come on, let's go people-watch."

"Are you sure I look all right?" Dianne asked, stopping Alex as he reached for the door of Callahan's Friday night. After some debate, she'd decided on a white cotton sweater, black pants, and a loose black-and-white scarf.

Alex kissed her on the forehead. "You look beautiful."

"I wasn't sure. I've never been on a pool date before."

"My first one as well, and you're also the first woman I've brought here."

"You know, Alex, this might be selfish again, but I'm so glad another woman didn't snap you up." She curved her arm through his and leaned into him. "You have a way of making me feel special."

"That's because you are."

Opening the door, they went inside. The mournful sounds of Maya, C. J.'s favorite singer, greeted them from the jukebox. His arm around Dianne, Alex led her to a booth in the back. She slid in, and he followed.

"What are you and the lady having, Alex?" a waitress called from across the way at another table.

"Beer and tonic water," he answered.

"Be back as quick as I can." She moved away with a tray of empty beer bottles and shot glasses.

Dianne tapped the RESERVED sign. "Do you ever have trouble getting a table?"

"Since I don't go out that much, no," he answered.

She frowned at him. "This is New York."

He glanced away. "I still prefer staying at home."

"Yet you're taking me out."

He picked up her hand. "And enjoying it. I never had a reason before."

"We're staying in tomorrow night," she told him.

"And miss the helicopter ride over the city?" he said. "I hear it's very romantic."

She leaned toward him. "With you, everything is romantic."

He kissed her lightly on the lips.

"Well, well. Summer was right on." C. J. placed the drinks on the table.

Dianne looked up to see a tall, gorgeous, clean-shaven man with linebacker shoulders and close-cut curly black hair in a T-shirt and jeans. He stuck out his hand. "C. J. Callahan."

Dianne took the callused hand, found hers almost swallowed. "Pleased to meet you."

"Same here."

Alex separated their hands. "Enough."

C. J. grinned. Dianne hugged Alex's arm.

"So, I'm possessive."

"With good reason." C. J. slid into the booth across from them.

"Why, thank you," Dianne said with a smile.

"Looks like you hit it out of the park, Alex."

Dianne looked around to see another gorgeous man with a chin-strap beard and twinkling black eyes. He extended his hand.

"Payton Sinclair. Friends call me Sin."

Chuckling, Dianne took his hand, surprised to feel calluses before pulling her hand back. "I can see why."

"Smart woman you have, Alex." Sin stared down at C. J. "Move over."

C. J. scooted out of the booth. "I might have to help. A certain sport consultant said he was meeting some athletes at Callahan's tonight in a radio interview this morning."

"You can thank me later." Sin pointed toward Alex's beer. "You gonna drink that?"

Alex pushed the longneck toward him. "You know C. J. likes to keep the place low-key."

"I also know a leggy brunette sports reporter just

might drop by." Sin tilted the bottle. "She asked about you, C. J."

C. J.'s grin was slow and easy. "You might make it out of here in one piece."

"Noted." Sin pulled the beer nuts in front of him. "Man, I'm hungry." He looked at Dianne. "How about we get out of here and grab a bite to eat."

Dianne's mouth gapped. Annoyed, she looked at Alex. "I thought he was your friend."

"Don't mind Sin." Alex draped his arm across Dianne's shoulder, "His mind works so fast his mouth gets ahead of his brain."

"We tolerate him," C. J. added.

Sin swallowed the beer nuts. "Don't let them fool you. They are just annoyed because I whipped them the last time we played pool. I plan to do it again tonight. Right after I get something to eat."

"Here you are, Sin." A hamburger and onion rings plopped on the table along with a bottle of ketchup and a draft beer.

"Thanks, Piper. Please bring Alex a replacement." Sin picked up an onion ring, shoved the plate across the table to Dianne. "They're the best in the city."

Dianne had never met anyone who seemed to jump so quickly from one topic to another. But if he was Alex's friend, he must be all right. "I shouldn't."

Alex snagged one, bit it, and offered it to Dianne. She immediately took a bite, then reached for the remaining part to finish it off. Alex signaled Piper. "Another onion ring and burger."

"So how did you two meet and, if you dump him, can I call you?" Sin bit into his burger with relish.

Dianne finally caught on. "I never settle for second best."

Sin choked. C. J. happily slapped him on the back, grinning for all he was worth. "I guess she told you."

"She sure did." Sin nodded at Alex. "She's a keeper."

Alex kissed her on the head. "I already know that."

"As soon as Sin finishes stuffing himself, we can play," C. J. said. "I already put a sign up that the table is reserved from nine until."

Alex nodded toward the door. "Neither of you might be playing tonight. The reporter is here and looks like she has a friend."

C. J. and Sin both jerked their heads around to stare over the back of the booth. Two beautiful women stood near the door. C. J. was moving and Sin, his food forgotten, was right behind him. Almost immediately the star pitcher for the Yankees came through the door with his agent, and with him several fans. At least for a while, Alex would have Dianne to himself, and he was going to enjoy every second.

Chapter 7

Alex could be annoyed or he could just enjoy having Dianne leaning back against him as they watched Sin try to teach Heather, the friend of the sports reporter C. J. was interested in, how to pocket a shot. Soon after the Yankee pitcher and agent arrived, so did several other baseball payers, along with their agents and reps from corporations eagerly trying to court them. It had been wild.

New patrons at Callahan's had been agog, trying to get pictures and autographs. The regulars had taken it all in their stride. Unlike usual, C. J. wasn't frowning. Carol, the sports reporter they'd met last week at the Yankees game, kept a smile on his face.

Sin had done his thing of bringing player, agent, and corporation together in a nonthreatening environment. The reporter had gotten her interviews and couldn't have been happier. Alex could already tell C. J. would reap the reward of her appreciation.

It was close to ten before the players, reps, and agents left and the bar returned to normal. It was Sin's idea to pair off so two couples could play against each other;

the winner would play the third couple. He didn't seem to mind that Carol's friend, Heather, had never played pool before.

The giggling redhead needed help with everything. After five practice shots, she still couldn't hold her pool cue without Sin's help. Carol was almost as bad with C. J. Alex couldn't believe that a woman who loved sports as much as she said she did had never played pool.

The ball Sin helped Heather hit knocked a ball into the side pocket. Heather screamed with joy, jumping up and down, her breasts joggling. Sin grinned.

Dianne turned to stare up at Alex. He couldn't say he wasn't looking at Heather's obvious attributes. He rubbed his brow.

Alex heard choked laughter and stared at C. J. nearby. He'd seen the exchange and was amused.

"We're going to win when we start playing for real," Sin announced casually, his arm around Heather's small waist as she leaned into him. "Your practice shot, Dianne."

Dianne took the cue from Alex and marched stiff-backed to the pool table. Alex followed. He couldn't tell if she was annoyed at him for looking at Heather or annoyed that she had yet to sink one ball. He was to blame for both.

He wasn't the best of pool players, but with Dianne's soft hips against him, his thinking and concentration were mush.

Without waiting for him, Dianne bent over the table. The material of her slacks tightened over her hips. Alex swallowed.

"Buddy, she's aiming her cue at Sin's ball," C. J. said casually.

Heather went into a fit of giggles. Alex caught the strained smile on Sin's face. Alex thought someone should have told her that a lot of men didn't like helpless, giggling women. He looked at Dianne, her hand on her hip, her mouth tight. Oops. Maybe someone should have told him that a woman didn't like a man who said he cared about her looking at another woman.

Alex took the cue with one hand and wrapped his arm around Dianne. "You. Just you."

Her face and body softened. "What do you say we get out of here and go for a carriage ride?"

Alex tossed the cue to C. J., who caught it. "'Night, everyone."

"Good night." Dianne curved her arm around Alex's waist.

"You were going to tell me about the new D line," Heather protested, moving away from Sin. Carol was behind her.

Dianne briefly glanced up at Alex. "Sorry. I'm sure you'll understand."

Alex didn't particularly care if they did or not. He was taking his woman and leaving.

"I always thought this would be nice," Dianne said, snuggling closer to Alex on the carriage seat as it went down Madison Avenue heading for Central Park.

"Same here." He nuzzled her neck. "You smell good."

"So do you." He laughed and she sat up to look at him. "What?"

He threaded his hand through her soft hair. She was sensually beautiful and so unaware of it.

"What?" she repeated.

"We sound like a mutual admiration society," he mused.

"Just proves we have good taste." She leaned back against him, wrapping her arms around the strong arms that now circled her waist. "It's beautiful with the lights in the trees, the buildings. I guess I never took time to appreciate New York."

"Most people who live in the city are the same way," Alex said. "Jobs, friends, family, obligations keep most people pretty busy."

"I get two out of four," she said, trying to sound cheerful. He wasn't buying it.

"The D line solidified the House of Harrington as an innovative fashion leader. You helped make that happen," he reminded her.

"The job is all I have," she whispered softly.

His heart ached for her. She sounded so alone, so scared. This time he was the one turning her face to his. "Is everything all right at Harrington House?"

Her lashes flickered. She glanced away. He gently shook her. "Dianne. I asked you a question."

Finally she returned his gaze. By the lights from the streets and buildings, she knew he could see the strain in her face. "They're late with my paycheck again."

"Again?" he shouted. "How late? How many times? Why didn't you tell me?"

Her shoulders snapped back in defiance. "Because I

can take care of myself. I spoke with the CEO's secretary and they'll have my check at the meeting Monday."

Despite her words, he could tell she was worried. So was he. But he had to tread carefully. Because she'd been told so many times by her unfit parents that she was stupid, she bristled when anyone inferred she couldn't take care of herself. "Perhaps I should be at that meeting."

"No. I already told them if they didn't have my check, they'd be talking to my lawyer." She poked him in the chest. "I figured you'd tear them a new one."

"Damn straight. When you're at the meeting, don't you dare leave without a contract. Make the CEO put the basis in writing," he told her.

She saluted him. "Yes, sir."

The harshness faded from his face. He'd let her handle things, but if they continued to screw her over with her paycheck, they'd have him to deal with. "Smarty."

"It will be fine, I promise." She leaned back against him. "You off tomorrow?"

"Yep. We can spend the entire day together starting with breakfast and then the baseball game at Yankee Stadium. If the Yankees win, Sin invited us to an early dinner with a group of his corporate clients at Radcliffe's," Alex told her. "Since I'm closer to the stadium and Radcliffe's, if you'd like you can bring a change of clothes over in the morning and come back to my place to dress for dinner."

She popped back up, her eyes dancing with excitement and just a bit of nervousness. He'd said he would want her to spend the night when they made love for the first time. Tomorrow night she'd be in Alex's bed. "Thank you. I'd like that."

Alex felt her pulse leap. She understood he planned for her to spend the night. "After I pick you up, we can drop your things at my place on the way to the game."

"I haven't been to a baseball game since yours in high school. You were a great pitcher."

"I still have a strong arm." He pulled her closer.

"Show me."

"With pleasure." His mouth found hers.

Dianne expected them to sit in the bleachers for the Yankees baseball game; instead they were shown to an elegant box that must have cost thousands. "Sin," she guessed.

Alex grinned. "He has his good points."

Inside the luxurious room, she spotted Sin deep in conversation with two men. She didn't recognize them, but then she hadn't known any of the sports figures last night at the bar, either. "Is C. J. coming?"

"He's probably already here. I'm usually the last to arrive," Alex said. "I don't see him, but I do see the buffet."

"You're wicked, you know. I've lost only one pound."

He leaned over and whispered in her ear, "I'll give you a private workout later on."

Dianne's cheeks flamed with excitement. "I'm going to hold you to that."

Hand in hand they went to the buffet table. As the crowd moved away, Dianne saw Summer at the head of one of the tables. "Hi. I didn't expect to see you here. I thought you'd be at the restaurant."

"I would be if Sin hadn't asked me to cater. We're booked solid as usual." Summer picked up a china plate. "Would you like me to serve you?"

"No. We have it." Dianne took the plate. Sin was a good friend. "Not that you need it, but the publicity has to be good for Radcliffe's."

"It is." Summer made a face. "He has his moments—brief though they may be."

"We must be talking about Sin." C. J. picked up a plate.

"You and Carol lost," Alex guessed, picking up flatware.

C. J. grunted and reached for the utensil in the potato salad. "I'll get him next time."

"Men and their games." Summer added thin slivers of roast beef and garden salad to C. J's plate. "You were sure you were going to win. What happened?"

"I was distracted." C. J. plucked the fork from Alex's hand and dug into his food.

Dianne looked at Alex, who became busy preparing their plate.

"A woman." Summer folded her arms. "Is she here?"

"No way. You know game day is sac—" C. J. broke off abruptly, his gaze zeroed in on Dianne, then Alex.

"Finish what you were going to say," Dianne told him, although she had a pretty good idea.

"C. J.," Alex said. His voice carried a note of warning.

"I was going to say game day is sacred for me, Sin, and Alex. We don't bring women, but since you're here, obviously you're just not any woman. You're important to him, and therefore important to us," C. J. said.

Dianne hugged him, or at least tried to. Alex pulled her away.

"I saw that," Sin said, joining them. "If C. J. gets a hug, as your other best friend I get one as well."

Dianne only got one arm around Sin's neck before Alex pulled her to his side. "That's enough."

"Spoilsport." Sin picked up a plate. "It's a good thing I have a thick skin. You and the food are looking good, Summer. Radcliffe's is going to be even more popular."

"Who was the woman?" Summer asked.

Sin glanced up from peering at a huge clamshell filled with giant shrimp. "Forgettable. Some women are."

Dianne glanced from Sin to Summer, trying to determine if anything was going on between them. Sin hadn't been teasing and hadn't mixed two completely different subjects when he'd answered her. Alex hadn't seemed to notice, but C. J.'s brow was furrowed.

"There just better not be another incident like last time," she said, and stalked away.

Sin's expression changed. For once, he seemed deadly serious. Placing the plate on the table, he went after her.

C. J. muttered an expletive, took a step toward them, then went to take a seat at the front of the box, which looked out over the infield.

Dianne didn't want to be nosy, but she liked Summer. "Is she all right?"

"Sin won't rest until she is," he answered cryptically.

Still frowning, Dianne stared at Sin and Summer. They made a beautiful couple, but Dianne didn't think they were or ever had been one. Moments later, Summer laughed, punched Sin playfully on the shoulder. Whatever it was, it was over.

"I have our plate, let's go take our seats. The game is about to start."

"I'm the first, huh?" Dianne asked.

"And only." Alex nodded toward C. J.

Dianne started toward C. J., but she was still thinking about what Alex had said. *And only.* She hadn't thought about it before, but what if Alex expected more from her than she could give him? Not just sexually, but emotionally as well. She had told him what she wanted from him, but what about what he wanted?

She hadn't even thought to ask. That made her just as selfish as she'd said.

Alex had always given to her and, as usual, she had taken without a moment's thought about giving back, as if being intimate with her was enough.

Foolish woman.

He'd made each moment memorable, introduced her to his best friends. They obviously thought she was special in his life. What would they say when she went back to Paris?

An unexpected stab of loneliness hit her. She didn't want to leave him.

"Are you all right?" he asked.

"Fine," she managed, searching for and finding a real smile. Not for anything would she ruin this day for him or for herself. Memories of them together would have to last a lifetime.

* * *

The Yankees won, and New York celebrated as only the Big Apple could. Alex took Dianne back to his apartment so they could shower and change, then hurried back to Radcliffe's. They were immediately shown to Sin's table.

"I don't see C.J," Dianne said as they followed the hostess.

"Game days are always busy at his bar. He even has extra staff on hand. His regulars will be waiting for the bar to open. Today they'll be celebrating. If things had gone differently they'd be there to drown their sorrows. Big crowd either way."

"About time you got here. Now the party can begin." Sin came to his feet and introduced them, then turned to Summer who was standing by his side. "Ladies and gentleman, you've already met the beautiful and savvy owner of Radcliffe's, sampled her exquisite cuisine at the stadium. Now you'll understand why the wait list is two months, and people don't mind waiting for the off chance that someone will miss their seating time."

"Welcome to Radcliffe's," Summer said, and lifted her hand. Four waiters appeared. "They'll take your orders and, in the meantime, please enjoy the wine and appetizers Mr. Sinclair ordered."

Alex watched the pleased and impressed faces of executives who were used to the best restaurants. Sin, with Summer's help, had nailed it again. It was good to see that they had managed to get over the bump at the stadium, but until they got it out in the open and put things firmly behind them, it would continue to pop up.

"I'll be back and forth, but if there is anything you

need to make your dining experience more enjoyable, please let me know." Summer turned to leave.

Frowning, Sin caught her arm. "You can't stay?"

Something flickered in her face, then was gone. "Unfortunately not. Good-bye for now."

Sin was forced to release her arm. Alex was sure he was the only one who could tell by the sudden narrowing of his eyes that Sin hadn't wanted to release her. He could be difficult when pushed, and Summer was definitely pushing him.

"Is this your first time at Radcliffe's?" Alex asked the man seated next to him to draw attention away from Sin.

The man was in his midthirties and wearing a well-cut suit; he picked up his just-filled wineglass. "Yes, but it certainly won't be the last if the food is anything like it was at the stadium."

"It is," Dianne said. "The food and service are fantastic. Unfortunately, I'll have to forgo the wine tonight."

"Excuse me, but are you *the* Dianne Harrington?" a matronly woman asked.

"Yes," Dianne admitted, then smiled. "And might I say you look fantastic in that D suit."

The woman blushed with pleasure. "Thank you. I love your clothes. They're stylish and they last."

"Not that that keeps her from buying more clothes," her husband said with obvious indulgence.

"Your appetizers." As several platters were placed on the table, people turned their attention to the food.

As the evening progressed, Dianne fielded almost as many questions about fashion and the fashion industry as Sin did on the execs' chances of acquiring the particular sports figure they wanted to endorse their brand. Alex had never been prouder of her.

And tonight she was going to be his.

Dianne had never been as anxious in her life. Her heart thudded in her chest; her palms were damp. What if she was a complete failure in the bedroom? What if, when Alex saw her naked, he'd think she was too fat?

Alex stuck the key in his apartment door, his gaze on Dianne. "We still have time to take the helicopter ride if you want?"

"No." She shook her head. When he'd asked about the ride as they were leaving the restaurant, there had been no hesitation: She wanted to return to his apartment. She still did—it was just . . .

Alex removed the key from the door, caught both her arms, and waited until she stared up at him. "You never have to do anything you don't want to."

"But I want to," she blurted, then looked away.

Releasing her, Alex opened the door. Gently taking her arm, he led her inside.

"Oohhh," she whispered. The room was filled with the intoxicating scent of roses and gardenias. On several surfaces were candles. With the draperies open, the light from the building coupled with the candles gave the room a warm, romantic glow.

He stepped behind her, his arms going around her waist. "I hope you approve."

"Very much." She leaned back against his muscular warmth.

He rubbed his cheek against hers. "I wanted our first time to be special and memorable."

Excitement rushed through her. She shivered.

Alex straightened. He stepped away and hit the light switch. Light flooded the room. Frowning, she whirled on him.

"The evening is still young," he said casually. "What would you like to do?"

He was giving her a choice. She walked over and flipped off the light. "I want to make love with you. I was nervous because I might disappoint you."

"Honey." He said the word with reverence, then took her gently into his arms. "Never. I told you that you are a fantasy that I never allowed myself to believe would be mine."

"I don't want it to turn into a nightmare," she said, trying to sound teasing and failing miserably.

"I had planned for us to wait, but I think it's best I show you just how much you mean to me." His head bent, his mouth gently settled over hers, letting the heat and need grow. Molding his mouth to hers, he let his tongue lazily lap against hers.

Dianne felt her breath leave her as she sank deeper into the kiss, letting the rising sensation push away her fear, replacing it with a flickering flame of desire that grew as his hand worked its way beneath her jacket and brushed against her bare skin. Her hands clutched his arms, felt the muscles bunch.

"Your skin is like the softest velvet," he murmured as he ran a thumb over her tight nipple.

Heat and need spiraled through her. She wanted to touch him as well.

Her fingers quickly unbuttoned his shirt. By the time she was finished he had his jacket off, his belt unbuckled. She pressed her hands against the muscled warmth of him, then her lips, and felt him jerk.

Her head came up. She couldn't see his eyes clearly, but his breathing had altered. She'd done that. "I'm not scared anymore."

"You may have saved my sanity." He laughed.

She laughed with him, feeling freer than she ever thought possible, and it was all due to the man standing before her. "This feels so right."

"Honey," he said, his mouth finding hers. This time there was nothing gentle about the kiss; it was bold and daring and demanding.

Dianne felt her jacket leave her arms, felt desire rise as he clamped his arm around her waist, drawing her against him. He bent her backward, his mouth fastening to her aching nipple. Air hissed though her teeth. She felt the sucking sensation deep inside her. Moaning, she clutched his head to her.

His head lifted. His breathing ragged. This time she could see his eyes. They were dark with desire and an inner fire that called to her. "Alex."

Sweeping her up in his arms, he went to the bedroom at a quick clip when he wanted to run, would have if there had been more light. He had never wanted, needed like this. He'd always known it would be different with Dianne; he just hadn't known how much. He wasn't even inside her body, but just the thought had him teetering on the edge.

Stepping into the bedroom, he heard her sigh his name. He tried to see it though her eyes—the soft glow of candles on the dresser and night chest. A huge bouquet of roses and gardenia blossoms on a table. A bottle of Perrier-Jouët chilling in an automatic champagne server. The covers of his bed pulled back with white rose petals sprinkled on top.

He felt dampness against his chest, and quickly set her to her feet to stare at her. "Are you all right?"

"Better than I ever thought possible." She sniffed. Circling his waist, she leaned against him and gazed around the room. "This took thought and planning."

He tilted her chin upward to stare into her teary eyes. The flowers had been delivered before he went to pick her up. He'd personally sprinkled the rose petals. He wished the candles were real instead of battery-operated and on timers. One day they would be.

"There's more, but for now . . ." He kissed her, tasting the sensual sweetness and passion that was uniquely hers. Lifting his head, he picked her up and went down on the bed with her. The scent of the roses wafted around them. With their faces inches apart, their hands locked, their breath mingling, he wanted to tell her he loved her, but realized that would have to wait. She wasn't ready to believe him. She'd think he was caught up in the moment. He could show her, though.

Straddling her, he unclasped her bra, then stared in reverence. "You're exquisitely beautiful." He tasted her skin, curled his tongue around her nipple. Moving lower, he unfastened her skirt and, standing, tugged it from her body.

His throat dried. His heart raced on seeing the first hint of her lace panties. Mercy. His hands trembled so much he had to grit his teeth to have enough composure to pull her skirt from her body. Finished, he gazed at her, beautiful and exquisite and his.

Quickly he finished undressing and crawled back on the bed over her. "You're all that I desire," he breathed, then began raining kisses over her body. His hand worshiped her until she was twisting restlessly beneath him.

Quickly sheathing himself, he slid his hands beneath her hips and entered her. The fit was tight, exquisite. He felt the resistance of her body, reached between them and found the sensitive nub and flicked his thumb again and again. He flexed his hips, going deeper. His mouth clamped on hers as he bought them together again and again.

It was almost too much. She hadn't known desire could take you under so fast, so completely. All she could do was hold on, revel in the power and the passion of the man loving her so completely that tears stung her eyes. She felt something coil tight inside her, tried to pull back. He wouldn't let her. He surged forward, faster, deeper, stroking, compelling her to let go of the control she'd always prized.

This time when the coiling sensation began deep inside her, she reached for it, embraced it. The orgasm tore through her. She locked her arms around his damp back, her legs tightening around the hips pumping into her, and held him tightly. His arms were even tighter around her, holding her as he reached his own pleasure.

As she came down, one word came to her. "Bliss."

"Bliss," he repeated, nuzzling his cheek against hers before rolling and taking her with him. His hand threaded though her hair. He smiled.

"What?"

"I dreamed of your hair on my pillow," he said.

Leaning up, she climbed on top of him. "I've had a few dreams myself."

"Keep that thought." Gathering her tenderly in his arms he started for the bathroom. "You need some time in the Jacuzzi, and since I don't want to be away from you, we'll go in together."

Happier than she ever thought possible, she leaned into him as he turned the faucets on and water gushed into the Jacuzzi. "Taking care of me?"

Shutting off the water, he kissed her on the forehead. Then with her in his arms he stepped into the swirling water. "Always."

She was driving him slowly out of his mind, and he was enjoying every second. They'd no more than returned to his bed than she had pushed him down on his back and began to kiss and nip her way over his body. When she'd taken him inside her, he'd had to grit his teeth and grip her slim waist to maintain control.

Then she'd started to move, and he'd lost it. Pleasure swamped him. His body deep inside hers, she rode him, satisfied him. He watched the intense pleasure on her face, felt a wild exhilaration that he had put the look there.

She was shameless and reveled in it. Her hands on his muscled chest, her eyes half closed, her head thrown back, she met his demands and made demands of her own. Pleasure and need drove her. She wanted to give back to him as he'd given to her.

He quickened the pace. This time she knew what would happen. Her body tightened, her hands fisted. His hands held her as he reached his satisfaction at the same time.

Deliciously sated and tired, she lay on top of him, content and happy. "I never imagined it could be this good."

He turned her face to his. "Neither did I."

Smiling, aware of the gift he had just given her, she felt her heart stumble. *Please, don't make me fall in love with you,* her mind whispered, but she wondered if it was already too late.

"Wake up, beautiful." With a breakfast tray, dressed only in pajama bottoms, Alex approached his bed a little after ten Sunday morning. "Breakfast is here."

Dianne lifted her head from the pillow, blinked, then smiled. His heart knocked against his ribs. She got to him, and always would. With her hair tousled, her skin glowing, she was gorgeous and tempting. When she sat up, the sheet slid down over the creamy breasts he'd taken great pleasure in loving. His body immediately hardened.

"Please pull the sheet up or this will be stone-cold before we eat," he warned, his grip on the tray tightening.

With a teasing smile, Dianne tugged the sheet back up and scooted against the headboard. "If you hadn't looked so pleased with yourself, I might test your theory."

"Fact." He placed the tray over her lap, gave her a hot wet washcloth for her hands, then climbed in beside her. He lifted the domed top. Beneath was a large platter with soft scrambled eggs, cinnamon toast, pan sausages, bacon, and a fruit cup.

"Thank you." She blessed the food, then reached for the cup of steaming black coffee. "Why didn't you wake me to help?"

"Not necessary. I had it delivered. Lunch and dinner will be delivered as well." He reached for a slice of crisp bacon. "We're going to spend a leisure day in bed."

She sipped her coffee. "Good, because there are a couple of things I was thinking about doing with you."

He grinned. "I'm your man."

Chapter 8

Monday morning at 9:50 Dianne stepped out of the cab in front of the House of Harrington's office building for her 10:00 AM appointment. In a lemon-yellow silk suit, understated gold jewelry, and five-inch Chanel leopard-print heels with matching clutch, she couldn't help the smug, satisfied smile on her face. Her skin tingled. She could almost taste the last kiss Alex had given her before they'd left his apartment that morning.

Inside the building, still smiling, she stepped into the crowded elevator and noted that someone had already pushed the button for the eighth and top floor where the executive offices were located. Her thoughts easily returned to Alex. She'd just spent the most fabulous weekend of her life with a man who'd fulfilled her every desire and fantasy. In bed and out, Alex was everything she could have wanted in a lover.

He made her feel desirable, sensual. She now knew a little bit of the way Catherine felt with Luke—giddy with happiness and on top of the world.

But Catherine and Luke had forever. She and Alex just had tonight. Sadness hit her, but she shook it away.

She'd known from the beginning that this wouldn't last forever. They hadn't discussed the future. When she left for Paris tomorrow, that might be the end of it. Her stomach knotted at the thought of never again being in Alex's arms, or seeing him smile.

No wonder Catherine and Luke, no matter what, never spent the night apart. It was too painful otherwise. Once she returned to Paris, her schedule would be hectic with fittings, photo shoots, and interviews. She wasn't scheduled to return to New York until Fashion Week in September—three long months away.

"Excuse me."

Startled out of her musing, Dianne stepped aside, then followed the young woman who had spoken to her off the elevator. The first thing Dianne noticed was that the pictures of her grandparents, and then her grandfather, standing with the designers or models depicting the evolution of fashion at Harrington, were gone from the freshly painted wall. Anger hit her.

If the new CEO thought he could erase her grandparents' influence and memory, he'd thought wrong. Her parents had been in a couple of those pictures. They both liked being in the spotlight. Dianne was sure they'd insist their pictures be rehung. She didn't think they'd ask for those of her to be put back. It didn't matter. What mattered was that her grandfather's memory and legacy be preserved, just as he wanted.

Dianne went to the receptionist's desk across from the elevator. "Dianne Harrington to see Mr. Boswell."

A redhead with her black roots and too much cleavage showing glanced up. She didn't smile. "Good morning, Ms. Harrington. They're in the boardroom," the receptionist said. "Nancy will show you the way."

"Thank you," Dianne said to the stony-faced receptionist, wondering what had happened to Thelma, the usual receptionist who always had a smile and stories of her grandchildren.

"This way."

Although Dianne knew the way, she followed the young woman down the hall. Boswell probably wanted to show he was in charge again. The straight-backed unsmiling woman she followed was the woman from the elevator and another new face.

Boswell had made noticeable changes in the New York office. Dianne's stomach knotted with apprehension. She forced herself to relax. She had nothing to worry about. Her parents had a controlling interest in Harrington. As she'd told Alex, they valued money and the D line was selling well.

Thinking of Alex again brought a smile to her face, and an embarrassing tightening of her nipples. It was a good thing she was walking slightly behind the other woman. Dianne promised herself that, as soon as the meeting was over, she'd call Alex and see if he could get off early. She wanted to spend every possible moment with him until her plane left for Paris tomorrow.

"Here we are." Stopping at a door in the middle of the hall, the woman knocked briefly then opened the door and stood to the side for Dianne to enter

"Thank you." Dianne's smile warped into the *World*

be damned confident runway look that said she owned the universe and everything in it. She stepped past the young woman.

The first thing she noticed was there were only four people at the large table, which seated twelve. The second thing was that her parents didn't even look up from studying the contents of the open blue binder in front of them. The third and most daunting fact was that the new CEO wore the same *be damned* look.

"Good morning," she said.

Her parents, elegant and remote, finally glanced up. They didn't return her smile. "Hello, sweetheart."

"Hello, dear."

The muscles in Dianne's stomach tightened. Her parents were in their on-camera mode. When that happened, she always got the shaft.

"Good morning, Ms. Harrington, I'm Ms. Hill," said the tall, slim middle-aged brunette sitting beside the remaining person in the room. "Mr. Boswell, the CEO."

"Ms. Harrington, please have a seat," Boswell said with as much warmth as an icicle. Dressed in a tailored blue suit, he appeared to be in his midsixties, with salt-and-pepper hair, a strong, angular face, and eyes that revealed nothing. He didn't bother to stand.

This isn't good. She looked at her parents for reassurance, and received none. They were perfectly groomed in the latest fashion, elegant and gorgeous and as self-centered as they came. They made a good pair.

Dianne remembered how scared she'd been at her first runway show. Her grandfather hadn't been able to soothe her. A few of the seasoned models tried to help, but nothing could calm her—until her grandfather handed her the phone. It had been Alex, wishing her luck. While she was talking to him, she'd received a huge bouquet of white roses and gardenia blossoms.

She thought of the rose petals on the bed Saturday night and floating in the tub last night. She'd held her head high after she'd gotten off the phone with Alex before that first runway show, stopped looking at her feet and pranced. She did the same now, taking a seat opposite her parents, tilting her sunshades up on her head. And waited.

Boswell nodded to the blue binder in front of her. It had HOUSE OF HARRINGTON ANNUAL REPORT stamped on the front. "Please open it and turn to page twenty-six."

Ordering her hands not to tremble, she did as he asked. Dreading what she'd find, she slowly turned the pages. Her grandfather had taught her how to read the report. He wanted at least one member of the Harrington family to always control the company and know how to run it. He'd given up hoping that it would be his only child and son.

Her eyes zeroed in on the final numbers. She sagged in relief. Harrington House continued to make a profit even in difficult times. She glanced up with a smile. No one smiled back. "We're making a profit."

"Do you know how many people Harrington employs?" Boswell asked, leaning forward to put his arms on the table. He wore Tom Ford.

"Two hundred and seventy-five when Granddad ran the company," she said promptly, and watched surprise flicker across his face. Then it was gone.

"Each of those people expects a paycheck," he told her.

"And they get one," Dianne snapped. "Granddad took care of his employees. They were more than numbers, they were the heart and soul of Harrington House. He understood that he couldn't do everything, that he needed people who cared about Harrington and took pride in their jobs. My granddad was respected and loved."

Boswell's eyes, dark and cold, narrowed. He hadn't liked that. *Good.*

She could understand why her grandfather admitted to her that he regretted taking the company public to raise capital when she was no more than an infant. He hadn't liked answering to people. When profits began to climb, he'd begun buying back shares until he owned 55 percent. He'd given 10 percent jointly to her parents before she was born.

She and her grandfather had never talked about his remaining shares. He had talked of changing his will so the company would be in the hands of someone who cared, but he never had. No matter his intention or wishes, her grandfather had left his remaining 45 percent jointly to her parents.

"Not enough," Boswell finally said. "The board and shareholders want results and I intend to give it to them."

Dianne tensed. Her gaze flickered to her parents. She fully expected them to perk up at the mention of money. They looked down at the binders again. Odd. They'd never been interested in the annual reports. Their reading material consisted of fashion magazines for her mother and golf magazines for her father.

"I'm flying back to Paris tomorrow to work with René on the new D line. Buyers are already asking about what's in store," she said. "The marketing firm we hire can rev up a campaign to create a buzz."

"We," he said, straightening. "I wasn't aware that you owned any stock in Harrington House."

Dianne flushed, but she held her head up. "I'm a Harrington."

"You have traded on that long enough." He slid the binder away from him as if distasteful.

Hurt, incensed, Dianne jerked up in her seat. "How dare you."

"Dramatics," he scoffed. "You might have the name, but you're just a paid employee. An overpaid one in my opinion."

She jerked her head to her parents. Surely they'd say something to defend her. She'd worked for the past fourteen years helping to build the company, living out of suitcases, having few friends.

Nothing. They wouldn't even look at her.

"You're just another woman who thinks she can trade on her looks forever." Boswell, his eyes hard, leaned back in his seat. "No more."

Her gaze snapped to him. "What?"

"As of this moment, you're fired."

For a moment she couldn't breathe. She felt the room swirl and gripped the arms of the chair she sat in. "What?"

"Harrington doesn't need you. I've hired a new 'face.' One who is ten years younger and twenty pounds lighter," he scoffed. "Just look at you. No wonder sales aren't climbing."

She winced and finally found her voice. "You—you can't. Mother and Father have controlling interest in the company. Tell him. Mother. Father."

Their silence and refusal to meet her gaze sliced through her like a blade.

"Paulette."

The woman sitting next to him rose, placed an envelope in front of her, and returned to her seat.

"Your formal termination letter. Please leave your company cell phone, credit card, and penthouse key."

Dianne leaned back in her chair.

"Leave everything on the table. You'll find your clothes packed and ready for you," Boswell said. "I want you out within the hour."

Dianne rose on trembling legs. This couldn't be happening to her. "My money. You owe me."

"Harrington House owes you nothing. Your last check, a severance check, was used to pay a company for packing your things here and in Paris," he said with entirely too much satisfaction. "If you want those things you'll have to pay to ship them, but I'd do it quickly. I understand there was only enough money to pay for a month's storage. Your things here will be waiting for you."

They'd taken everything. She took a halting step.

"Credit card, cell phone, and penthouse key," Boswell repeated. "I wouldn't want to have to call security to obtain them, but I will."

Opening her purse, she removed her cell phone, credit card, and penthouse key and placed them by the letter. Gripping her handbag with both hands, she turned to go.

"Your departure is truly best for the company," he continued. "Your parents certainly see it that way."

Keep walking, she told herself. *Leave with some dignity.* But she found herself turning to her parents. "Please," she begged, unable to keep the tears from streaming down her cheeks. "Don't do this to me."

"It's best for the company," her father mumbled, barely glancing at her.

"What about what's best for me?" she hurled.

Annoyance flickered in her mother's eyes. "Don't make a scene, Dianne. You weren't at the company penthouse last night, so you have options."

Make a scene. Options. Dianne stared in disbelief at her parents. No, not parents. The people who had conceived her. Her gaze moved to the CEO who had just ruined her life and tossed her on the street, and the impassive woman, his secretary, by his side. She'd known Dianne was being fired and strung her along with empty promises. Without the apartment and with no credit card to check into a hotel, she was homeless.

She had nothing and no one.

And none of them in the room gave a damn. Lifting her head, she left without a backward glance and absolutely no idea what to do or where to go.

Alex was worried. Sitting at his desk in his office, he tried to concentrate on the contract in front of him, but it was difficult. He'd always been concerned that Dianne didn't have a contract, and that concern grew after the death of her grandfather. Knowing that she hadn't been paid increased his worry.

Dianne might think her parents' controlling interest gave her leverage, but he knew it didn't. They'd sell her out at the first opportunity. The new CEO was reputed to be a hard-ass. His focus was bottom line, not people. If he thought Dianne expendable—

"The contract can't be that bad," Summer said.

Alex's head lifted. He stared across the desk at her. "It's not."

"Then why did you look as if you wanted to rip someone apart?" she questioned.

Summer and Dianne were becoming friends, but he was sure she didn't want anyone to know how uncaring and heartless her parents were. "Thinking about another situation." He stood. "Looks good. You and the chef both preserve your rights."

Summer crossed her long legs and remained seated. "You usually ask if I have any questions."

"Sorry. You have any questions?" He glanced at his watch.

"I'd ask the reason your mind is elsewhere, but I don't think I'd get a straight answer." She came gracefully to her feet. "I like Dianne. You two didn't have a fight, did you?"

"I'm glad, and we haven't had a fight."

Summer studied him for a long moment. "Well, something has you wound tighter than a cheap watch."

He met her gaze levelly.

"All right. If you had loose lips, you wouldn't be so successful. I'll get out of your way."

"See you later, Summer." Rounding the desk, he walked her to the door. "If his lawyer has any questions, he can call me."

She paused at the door. "I hope whatever is bothering you works out for you."

"Thanks." He closed the door as soon as she walked through, went to his desk and dialed, then frowned. The last time he'd called Dianne's cell phone his message had gone into voice mail. This time the automated message said the number had been disconnected. He couldn't shake the worry that something was terribly wrong.

He glanced at his watch again, then his schedule. Her meeting should be over by now. His next appointment wasn't until one—more than enough time to swing by Dianne's apartment and check on her.

Fighting tears, Dianne hailed a taxi. As soon as she gave the man her address, misery hit her even deeper. That was no longer where she lived. She'd been alone before, but she'd never felt this hopeless or worthless.

Fired, and her parents hadn't said one word in her defense. They valued money more than they did their own daughter. She should have remembered that. Trembling hands clutched the handbag in her lap. Where would she go? What would she do?

She felt tears slide down her cheek and angrily brushed them away. Crying would solve nothing. She just wished she knew what would.

"Eighteen dollars and seventy-six cents. Lady."

The impatient way the cabdriver said *lady* told her that probably wasn't the first time he'd asked for the fare.

Embarrassed, she fumbled to open her purse and wallet. Fear and foreboding streaked through her. There was a ten, a twenty, and a few ones. She'd planned to take the check today directly to the bank.

Your last paycheck was used to hire someone to clean out your place here and in Paris. Tears clogged her throat.

"Lady," the driver said, impatience in his voice as he glared at her.

She handed him the twenty and got out. She'd taken two steps before she realized that Mel the doorman hadn't opened the cab door for her. Even now he was ignoring her. She thought they were friends. Apparently his loyalties lay with the one paying the rent. Her head lifted.

"Hello, Mel."

He finally looked at her, or rather over her left shoulder. "Was there something you wanted?"

Her life back the way it had been. That wasn't going to happen. "No." Struggling to remain upright and not dissolve into a puddle of misery and tears, she walked past him and into the lobby. To one side was a mountain of designer luggage that she'd dragged across the country. She'd always been a bit proud of her matching pieces and the envious stares she'd received. She wasn't prideful now.

"Ms. Harrington, would you like a cab?"

Dianne whirled to see the concierge, James Henderson. His gaze was direct and impersonal, as it had always been. He wasn't just being helpful. He knew.

She thought of the twelve-odd dollars in her purse. "I . . ." She faltered.

James lifted his hand, and the doorman came rushing back inside. "Call Ms. Harrington a cab and see that she is loaded up."

He was tossing her out. They didn't care. What did she expect when her own parents never had? She should have remembered that she wasn't lovable.

"Good-bye, Ms. Harrington," James said, and started toward his desk on the other side of the room. She wanted to shout at him for being so smug and heartless.

"Dianne."

Her heart clutched. No, please no. Alex seeing her tossed out like an old shoe would be the ultimate embarrassment.

A warm, tender arm circled her waist. Gentle lips brushed across her hair. She wanted to sway against him, be safe in his arms. Then the shame hit her again. She straightened away from him, sucked up her tears, and turned. She wanted to smile, but couldn't quite manage it.

Alex wanted to pull her back into his arms, but for some reason he hesitated. He felt her withdraw from him and racked his brain for the reason. This morning she had been loving and all the woman he would ever need. Now she looked—fragile, lost.

She brushed her hair behind her ear. "What are you doing here?"

No kiss. No smile that brightened his world. "I couldn't get you on the cell, then when I called back it was disconnected."

The corners of her mouth lifted in a semblance of a smile. "Crank calls. I had the service disconnected."

"You didn't mention them before." He frowned, studied her closer. Were her eyelids a bit puffy? "I don't recall you receiving a lot of calls."

Her eyes blinked as if she were fighting tears. Then he wanted to kick himself. She had few friends. "Honey."

She evaded his touch and stepped back. Swallowed again. "My plans have changed. I was on my way to the airport." She glanced at the pile of luggage behind her. "My assistant got a bit carried away."

Alex looked from the luggage to her. She was upset and trying to hide it. "What happened in the meeting?"

She bit her lip, her smile faltering.

"Mr. Boswell. Welcome. The penthouse is ready for you and Ms. Easley to inspect."

Alex glanced behind him to see a middle-aged man with a thin woman no more than twenty hanging on his arm. Alex recognized the man immediately. The new head of Harrington.

As they started past them, the man stopped and stared at Dianne. "Glad to see you're being sensible," he said.

"The decorator is waiting as you instructed, Mr. Boswell. I'll personally take you up," the man who had greeted Boswell said, extending his arm toward the elevator.

It clicked for Alex. They were talking about Dianne's

place. The prick had fired her and put her out of her home. Alex wanted to go after the bastard, but Dianne seemed ready to shatter. He wanted to berate her for not calling him, but the vulnerability in her face—in her bleak eyes that had held so much laughter hours ago—wouldn't let him.

Instead he pulled a card from the inside of his coat pocket and wrote down his address. He motioned to a nearby security guard.

"If Ms. Harrington has any other belongings, please send them here." He gave the man a hundred. "I'd like that done today."

The money quickly disappeared into the man's pocket. "Certainly, sir. Anything else?"

"Two cabs should be enough for her luggage." He turned to Dianne as the man headed for the front. Alex gently took Dianne's arm, felt her tremble. "I'm here."

She didn't say anything. He had expected as much. Aware of her past, he knew she probably felt embarrassed, a failure. She wouldn't see it as a hard-nosed, unfeeling business decision delivered in the worst possible way by a man who only cared about the bottom line.

Outside, he helped her into a cab and took her cold hand in his. He wanted to hold her, but if he did he wasn't sure she wouldn't break down completely. Somehow he knew she didn't want to do that in front of him.

So he held her hand, stroked the back with his thumb, and contemplated planting his fist in the face of the bastard who'd fired her, getting her parents on the

D list for not backing their own daughter. All of that had to wait. Now his only concern was Dianne.

During the cab ride to his apartment, she didn't say one word or look at him. He ached for her and grew angrier by the second. "We're here, honey." He paid the driver, then helped her out. She refused to look at him and kept her head down, a sign of defeat and helplessness.

"Hello, Mr. Stewart," the doorman greeted, picking up as much luggage as he could.

"Thanks, Grant. Please see that the luggage is sent directly up. More is probably coming. You can put it in my personal storage for now," he told the man.

"Yes, sir."

In the elevator, Alex couldn't resist putting his arms around her. He wanted to tell her it would be all right. He realized that in her mind it would never be. "I'm here and I'm not going anyplace."

In his apartment, he steered her to the guest bedroom. He wanted her with him, but sensed her need to deal with the loss of her job alone. He opened the door and urged her toward the bed. "I'll put your luggage outside the door so it will be there when you need it. I'll work from home today so I'll be here if you need anything." Kissing her softly on the cheek, he closed the door.

He cursed all the way to his home office. He snatched up the phone and dialed his brother-in-law's office number.

"Man Hunters."

"Now I know how you felt when that man hurt Catherine."

"What happened, and how can we help Dianne?" came Luke's sharp response.

"She was fired without warning. She thought she was going to Paris tomorrow to work on a new line. Her luggage was packed and waiting for her when she got back to her apartment. The bastards couldn't have humiliated or embarrassed her more."

Air hissed though Luke's teeth. "You could beat the bastard to a bloody pulp, but it wouldn't change how she must be feeling now."

Alone. Miserable. Worthless. "Like I told Dad when that no-good jerk walked away from Catherine, it would make me feel better."

"If I ever see him, I'll give him a kiss from you."

Luke's voice was deadly quiet. Catherine's ex-fiancé had better hope he never crossed Luke's path. *Hurt my woman and watch your back forever.* Too restless to sit, Alex paced. "Find out what you can on Theo Boswell. I figure a man who is as cold and as heartless as he is has made a lot of enemies, enemies who might be itching to get back at him."

"I'm on it. You call Cath yet?"

"My next call."

"Understood."

He needed to set the wheels in motion to avenge the woman he loved and to calm down. "Let me know what you find out."

"I will. She might not want to hear it, but tell her we're here for her."

The more friends she had, the better. "I'll tell her." Disconnecting, he was about to call Catherine when there was a knock on the door. Answering, he instructed the man to put the luggage by the guest bedroom's door, waited, and then tipped him on the way out.

Alex knocked on the door. "Your luggage is here. I'll be in my office." Sure she wouldn't answer, he went to his office and called Catherine's cell.

Chapter 9

"Hi, big brother. This is an unexpected surprise."

"It's about Dianne." Perched on the corner of his desk, phone in hand, he told his sister everything. Catherine was as incensed and as angry as he'd known she would be. "This is the worst thing that could have happened to her."

"I know." Pushing away from the desk, he walked out onto the balcony. "She looks lost. I want to make this better for her and feel helpless that I can't."

"It's natural and normal," Catherine told him. "She'll have to work through this by herself. All you can do is be there for her."

"She's in the guest bedroom," he said, trying not to squirm.

"I'm proud of you. She needs time alone to process, to mourn, to be angry. It won't be easy to give her that time."

"I'm trying, but I want to—"

"Hold her, reassure her, kiss her."

He should have known he couldn't hide his feelings for Dianne from Catherine. "That about sums it up."

"Just be patient with her, as you've always been."

"Yeah."

"And Alex . . ."

"What else?"

"Knowing you and men in general, you probably haven't told her you love her."

He plopped down on a cushioned chair on the terrace and rubbed the back of his neck. "It's that obvious?"

"To me it is, because I love both of you. She's not ready to hear it now."

He came to his feet. That was just what he'd planned for later on that evening. "Catherine, I know you're the psychologist, but she needs to know someone cares."

"She's not ready. She'll think you feel sorry for her, that you're trying to bail her out again, save her," Catherine told him. "She'll resist. You've waited this long; a little while longer won't matter."

"I want to pound Boswell's face in until I feel better."

"It won't change things. You'll be in jail and who will be there for Dianne?" Catherine asked him. "She needs you this time more than ever before."

"I still want to hurt him and then her sorry excuse for a father," he said tightly, clutching the steel rail on the terrace. "A man shouldn't hit a woman, but I'd think of some retribution for her mother."

"Who or what is more important? Revenge or Dianne?"

"Dianne," he answered. She'd always come first. "I'm glad you're my baby sister even if you're smarter."

"I love you, too. I'd fly up there, but she'd not ready to see me."

Alex understood. Catherine's presence would be a reminder that she had it all: a man who was crazy about her, a secure career, a certain amount of fame and popularity. She had everything that Dianne had longed for and didn't have.

"Love you, too. I'll be in touch." Disconnecting, he called his office and advised his secretary to reschedule his appointments due to an emergency. In his home office, he replaced the cordless phone on his desk and went to the guest bedroom. The luggage was just as he'd left it. He knocked softly. Silence.

"Dianne."

He reached for the doorknob, then decided to get her a bottle of water. Her throat was probably dry from all the crying. Returning from the kitchen with the water, he knocked again.

He might not be able to tell her he loved her, but he wasn't going to let her hide from him. "I'm coming in, ready or not."

She was sitting on the side of the bed, stooped from the waist, her hands tightly clasped in her lap. *Defeated.* Trying to control his anger, he sat on the bed next to her. When their arms brushed, she flinched, trembled. *Scared.* Unscrewing the top, he held the bottle out to her.

Seconds turned into minutes. She continued looking down at her clenched hands. "I just spoke to Catherine."

Her head came up, her eyes wide, her lips trembled. "You can't tell her what happened."

His heart turned over. She looked so hopeless. "I don't know exactly what happened,"

Her head went down again. "I—I don't want . . ." Her voice faltered.

Why had the CEO fired her? Alex asked himself. The line was doing well. He'd have to wait to learn the answer. Dianne's well-being mattered more. However, if Luke found a way to make the CEO feel the same sense of fear and loss Dianne did, Alex would have no problem bringing the hammer down on his head.

Wanting to remind her that he'd always be there for her, he lightly curved his arm around her stooped shoulders. "You don't have to talk. I want to stay with you, but I can tell you want to be alone."

Her head downcast, she whispered, "Thank you."

He folded her hands around the bottle of water. "I'm going back to my office if you need me." Standing, he left the room, closing the door softly behind him.

Dianne had no idea how long she simply sat on the side of the bed, her head down, her thoughts in turmoil. She had no resources, no means of support. She couldn't stay with Alex. Every time he looked at her he'd see a failure. She couldn't stand that. But where would she go?

A knock sounded on the door. "Dinner's ready."

She'd never felt less like eating. She looked at the phone on the night chest beside her bed. Maybe she could get her parents to change their minds. She was their daughter. Maybe they'd had second thoughts.

"Dianne." The door opened. "Dinner's ready."

"Give me a minute, please."

"I'll see you in the kitchen."

Her hand trembling, Dianne placed the untouched

bottle of water in a small crystal tray on the nightstand and reached for the phone. Before she lost her nerve, she dialed her mother's cell phone number. As a former model, she'd understand what it meant to be fired, not to have a job.

Two, three, four rings, then her mother's recorded voice mail. "Astrid. Leave a message."

Dianne swallowed. "Mother, It's Dianne. I—I really need to talk. I need you and Daddy to get Boswell to change his mind. Please call me back when you get this message."

Dianne gave Alex's phone number and hung up. Her mother checked her cell phone messages regularly. She was too afraid of missing some juicy gossip or one of her salespeople calling about an event or a sale.

Another knock on the door. "Food is getting cold."

Alex was taking care of her again. What would she have done without him? She didn't even have cab fare, let alone a place to stay for the night. She glanced at the closed door. She wasn't hungry, but he wouldn't let it go until she ate something. Food finally wasn't high on her list.

A strange sound erupted from her lips. Now that she could eat all she wanted, she wasn't hungry. Laughter. High. Hysterical. She clamped her lips together. If she didn't stop, she wouldn't until she was a blubbering fool.

Too fat. Too old.

She winced as she recalled the CEO's harsh words. Her arms went around her waist. Embarrassment and fear engulfed her. She didn't want anyone to know, especially Alex.

"Dianne. I'm not eating without you."

Unsteadily, she rose to her feet. She was unsure of what she planned, but for now perhaps she could keep it light, playful. Being smart, he'd probably figured out she was fired. Thank goodness he didn't know the specifics. "Coming."

Looking around for her handbag, she picked it up and went to the bathroom. She always carried makeup. She glanced into the mirror and winced. The manufacture's claim of mascara not running proved true, but her face looked ravaged, her eyes bleak. She wasn't sure any amount of powder or rouge would help.

Reaching inside the bag, she repaired her makeup, put on fresh lipstick. Her hand trembled as much as her lips. Finished, she stared into the mirror. She wasn't sure she looked any better, but at least it gave her a bit more confidence to face Alex.

Taking a deep breath, she went to the door and opened it. Alex stood there with his right arm upraised, his eyes filled with concern and determination. Her lips began to tremble more. She wanted so badly to fling herself into his arms and let him fix the problem as he'd always done.

"Beef tenderloin, mashed potatoes, broccoli, and ice cream for dessert."

Some of her favorite foods. He'd remembered. No matter what, he had always been there for her. Dianne, the screwup who couldn't keep from making mistakes. He deserved better.

"Thank you, Alex. If you could call me a cab, I can get out of your way."

His eyes fired. The lips she'd loved to kiss and tease tightened. "Something wrong with my guest room?"

"Yes." She was letting him go first. She couldn't keep him. Soon he'd tire of her. Why should he want her? He was successful and she was a failure.

"All right." He picked up the smallest pieces of her luggage. "You can stay in my room. I want you with me anyway."

"What?"

He stopped and stared down at her. "Last night meant something to me. I thought it meant something to you as well. Was I wrong?"

She glanced away. "What has that to do with anything?"

"Being lovers moved us closer than ever. We're there for each other."

"I've never been there for you," she whispered, the truth of her words stinging her. Her head lifted. "I'm selfish."

He placed the luggage on the floor. His hands settled on her waist. "I told you once. I'll keep telling you until you believe. You're not selfish. You'd be there in a flash if I needed you. The opportunity just hasn't occurred yet."

She didn't feel better. "I'm a screwup."

"Not even close," he said tightly. "Life hasn't been easy for you. Despite that, you aren't cold or callous or a pain in the rear. You care about people."

"People just don't care about me," she murmured then tensed. She hadn't meant to say the words aloud.

"I care. So does Catherine. Now let's go eat."

"What about my cab?"

"Not happening." Taking her hand, he went to the kitchen. He hoped it was all right. He'd ordered a small bouquet of rose and gardenia blossoms with the food. "Have a seat. I'll get the food out of the warming oven."

He placed her plate in front of her, his on the other side of the table, and then he poured her a glass of red wine. "Once you eat, you can rest or watch a movie." He took a seat and blessed their food.

Dianne simply stared at her plate. The only sound in the room was the TV. He always watched the evening news. He felt helpless. It wasn't a feeling he was comfortable with. He searched his mind for something to say to make her feel better.

"There was a shake-up in the fashion industry today at the House of Harrington. Dianne Harrington, granddaughter of the founders and known as 'The Face,' was fired. Insiders report the model was overweight and beyond her prime."

Alex shot out of his seat, searching for the TV control at the first mention of Harrington. He didn't see it and cursed. The TV was in the wall. The manual controls were on the side and unreachable.

"Theo Boswell, the new CEO, hired newcomer Hillary Easley. In a prepared statement, Boswell says Ms. Easley has the youth, style, and body shape to take Harrington House to the next level of success."

Alex saw the control peeking from beneath the corner of a pot holder. He snatched it up and pressed POWER. He finally turned to Dianne. She looked shattered and lost.

"Dianne."

"I don't think I'm hungry." Getting up from the kitchen table, she went quietly to the guest bedroom and closed the door. Alex cursed long and hard.

Three days.

Dianne had been holed up in the guest bedroom for three days. At least while Alex was home. He'd given her a key the first night, but it was still on the dresser in the guest bedroom. He'd personally stocked the refrigerator with food. There was fresh fruit on the kitchen table. There were even chips and a couple of boxes of Godiva chocolate. As far as he could tell, Dianne had only drunk the bottled water from the refrigerator.

He started to his office to call Catherine but went to Dianne's room instead. He hadn't seen her since the morning after she'd arrived. She'd worn an oversized silk T-shirt. The instant she'd seen him, she'd quickly returned to her room.

He knew she was still there because he'd asked the door staff to notify him immediately if she tried to leave with her luggage. He'd snuck peeks into her room each night to check on her. Always she'd have the sheet over her head, as if even in sleep she didn't want to face the world.

But facing herself and the world was the only way to move on.

He knocked on the door. Waited. Nothing. Knocked again, then opened the door.

Dianne was in bed. The sheet was no longer over her head, but at her waist. Her hair was a tangled mess. She wore the same pale pink silk T-shirt. Empty bottles of water were on the night table.

It stopped today.

He crossed the room and shook her shoulder. "Dianne."

She jerked, then sat up in bed. Her eyes were bleak, her lids puffy.

"You need to shower, get dressed, and eat solid food."

"Go away, Alex." She reached for the sheet.

"Dammit, Dianne. Stop wallowing in self-pity and fight back."

Her lower lips trembled. Tears sparkled in her eyes.

His heart clenched, but he snatched her up in his arms. Her eyes widened.

"Put me down. I don't want to make love."

Alex didn't answer, just crossed the room to the bathroom and stepped into the shower. Placing her on her feet in front of the showerheads, he turned on the water full blast.

Dianne shrieked, cursed, fought him. He grabbed both of her flaying hands in his and let the water pelt her. After the longest two minutes of his life, he turned the water off.

"This stops today," he said. "Get cleaned up and start living your life."

"What life?" she said, tears and water flowing down her cheeks. "You heard the newscaster. I was fired."

"So what? You aren't the first model to lose her job and you damn sure won't be the last." He grabbed both of her shoulders and stared down into her miserable face. "You're more than a job. You're a special, beautiful woman. You're smart. You can be whatever you want."

"I don't know what I want," she sobbed.

"Then figure it out." He reached into his pocket, pulled out his wallet, and extracted his black American Express card. "I have important guests coming to dinner tonight, a couple from Atlanta. Buy whatever you need for dinner. They like beef. We'll be here at six."

"I can't. You know I can't," she wailed.

"Yes, you can. You just have to have as much faith in yourself as I have in you." He folded her trembling fingers over the card. "See you at six."

Sloshing in his shoes, he went to his room to quickly change. Shortly he was leaving again. Since the only water trail of footprints leaving the guest bedroom was his, she was still in the bedroom. He just hoped and prayed she came out swinging and not defeated.

She couldn't do this. She couldn't.

Dianne slid down on her butt in the enclosure and stayed there, leaning her head back against the tiled wall. Her life was a mess. If that wasn't enough, being told by the man you loved that you needed to take a shower wasn't the best way to start the day. But then her day had been going downhill since Monday. Three days!

It felt longer. A lifetime.

She felt the card clutched in her hand, and closed her eyes. She couldn't do it. She couldn't look herself in the mirror, let alone prepare a meal for four and entertain Alex's important clients.

She wiped at the tears streaming down her cheeks. The resounding question was: What *could* she do? She didn't like the answer that kept repeating in her head.

Nothing.

Her head fell forward until her forehead rested on her folded arms across her knees. She wished she could go back to the night they'd first made love. She couldn't remember when she'd been happier. She'd felt beautiful, sensual. Alex made her feel that way. He made her feel all the wonderful feelings she'd longed for and was so afraid she'd never experience. What had she done for him?

Nothing.

The truth ate at her, made her feel even more worthless. They hadn't been intimate because of her proposal, either. He'd made that clear. It was because he wanted her, had been attracted to her. She brushed water and tears from her cheeks. He liked her the way she was—kissed her in all the wicked places, worshiped her body. To him, she wasn't too fat or too old.

She squeezed her eyes shut. He knew her most embarrassing secret. Heck, the entire world knew she'd been fired because of her not-so-firm stomach, her flabby thighs, her big butt, her old age.

People would see her and think, *There's the fat, old woman.* She was a has-been at thirty-two. Her parents had certainly crossed her off their list. Neither had called her back.

Struggling up, she pulled off the T-shirt and turned on the water. She'd shower, dress, get her luggage, and get out of Alex's life. He deserved better, and no matter how much she wanted to be the woman he could be proud of, no matter how much she might wish otherwise, she wasn't that woman.

Alex tried to keep his fear from showing as he unlocked his apartment door a little after six that evening. He hadn't heard from Dianne since he'd left that morning. He had no idea what to expect. With him were Chuck and June Jefferson, two of his newest clients from Tyler, Texas. Mr. Jefferson's late father had been a land developer who had left his youngest son several valuable pieces of property in New York.

"It's nice of you to invite us to your home for dinner, Alex," Mr. Jefferson said. "After we left probate court this morning, we went sightseeing."

"And overdid," his wife said with an indulgent smile. "Someone should have warned us that your city blocks are nothing like those in Texas. I might not recover for weeks."

"The long blocks catch a lot of people unaware." Alex stepped inside so the middle-aged couple could enter.

"What a beautiful home you have, Alex," Mrs. Jefferson said, glancing around the living area. "And what a magnificent view."

"Inside and out," murmured her husband.

Alex followed the direction of his client's gaze, saw Dianne coming toward them with a tray of drinks, and grinned. He felt like pumping his fist in the air. She hadn't run. Crossing to her, he kissed her on the cheek and curved his arm around her waist. "Mr. and Mrs.

Jefferson, I'd like you to meet a very close friend of mine, Dianne Harrington."

"Please call me Dianne," she said and held out the tray. "Martini, light on the vermouth."

"Thank you. It's Dianne, if you'll call us Chuck and June," Mrs. Jefferson said, reaching for a glass and taking a sip. "Delicious."

Her husband sipped his drink. "Man, this hits the spot."

"Alex said you were in town on business, which can be a bit rushed," Dianne said. "Would you like to sit and enjoy your drinks or go into the dining room for dinner? It's beef Wellington."

The Jeffersons looked at each other, then faced Dianne. "Dinner," they said.

"Wonderful," Dianne said. "This way. You can bring your drinks, but if you'd like I have peach tea and coffee."

"This is too good not to finish," Mrs. Jefferson said as she walked beside Dianne. "But I think I'll have the peach tea. Our plane leaves at six thirty and I detest getting up early already without the added effects of alcohol."

"She's not her best until around eight." Mr. Jefferson chuckled. "The kids and I learned to walk easy in the morning."

"How many children?" Dianne asked as she placed the meat platter on the table.

"Five," they answered again in unison, then grinned across the table at each other.

"All of them are in law enforcement." Alex rounded

the table to help Dianne finish putting food on the table. "Mr. Jefferson's father pointed out to me several times that if I tried to fleece him, his grandchildren would be knocking on my door with handcuffs."

Mr. Jefferson stared down at his plate for a moment before lifting his head. "He hated that we and our children didn't want to move here and work with him, but he understood this wasn't for us."

"Father Jefferson was a great man." Mrs. Jefferson shook her head. "I'm proud of our children as well, but they've given me some bad moments."

"And you wouldn't change a thing," her husband said with conviction. "They enjoy helping others and they're good at what they do. No one could ask for anything more in a job."

Alex saw Dianne's smile waver, then firm. Afraid they'd ask Dianne what she did, he said, "You both have every right to be proud." He held Dianne's chair as she took her seat. Taking his own chair, he blessed the food.

"Do your children live near you?" Dianne asked, picking up her fork. She'd seen the concern in Alex's eyes a moment ago. She couldn't let him down with the first thing he ever asked her to do for him. She didn't know where life was headed, but she'd never be able to look herself in the face if she failed him.

"Now you've done it." Mr. Jefferson cut into his beef. "She'll talk for hours on the kids."

"You're just as bad," Mrs. Jefferson said. "They all live within a twenty-mile radius of us. Every Sunday, when possible, they all come over for dinner."

"And sometimes during the week," Mr. Jefferson pointed out.

"And when they don't, you call them on the phone wanting to know why." Mrs. Jefferson winked at Dianne and cut into her beef.

"I saw that," Mr. Jefferson said and turned to Alex. "You know one thing I've learned about women?"

"Probably the same thing I have. Nothing," Alex said.

"Always knew you were smart." Mr. Jefferson forked in another bite of beef. "And something else. You sure can pick 'em."

"My thoughts exactly, and might I say, you did a fantastic job yourself," Alex said.

With a raised brow, Mrs. Jefferson turned to Dianne. "Do they really think they did the picking?"

Dianne blinked, then smiled and picked up her glass. "To wise women everywhere."

Mrs. Jefferson picked up her glass and touched it to Dianne's. "To wise women."

Dianne sipped and placed her glass on the table, her gaze going to Alex across the table. She had picked him, and he had picked her right back. Loving Alex was the best decision she'd ever made. She never wanted him to regret that they'd been lovers. How she was going to accomplish that was beyond her as she smiled and chatted with his guests.

She just knew she'd never be able to live with herself if she didn't.

"You were fantastic," Alex said as soon as he returned from seeing the Jeffersons to a cab. Smiling, he caught

Dianne around the waist and pulled her to him. "I knew you would be."

Dianne simply stared at him. No matter what. He'd always be there for her, cheering her on. Her eyes stung with unshed tears. She blinked to keep them at bay. She'd asked for him to make her feel all the wonderful emotions of being loved. He'd done that and so much more.

"Honey." He tenderly kissed each eye. "It's going to be all right."

She wasn't so sure about the future, but there was one thing she had no doubts about. "Do you mind if you have company in bed tonight?"

His eyes fired. "I hunger for you. I wake up reaching for you. I go to sleeping aching for you."

Powerful emotions coursed through her. "Alex," she breathed. "You—" She sniffed, swallowed, tried to speak and couldn't get the words past the constriction in her throat.

"Dianne," he breathed, brushing his mouth, once, twice across hers before settling, deepening the kiss, his tongue searching inside her mouth as he pulled her against him, letting her feel the hard proof of his desire.

Her body caught fire in an instant. She pressed against him, eager for the magic and forgetfulness of his touch. His hand moved over her breast, causing need to ripple through her. Her hands clutched his shoulders.

The room tilted as he picked her up. All she could think of was *hurry*.

Alex had never wanted, needed so badly. Setting Dianne on her feet, he made himself slow down and unzip the front zipper of her dress when he wanted to rip. Drawing the material over her head, his heart stopped, then thudded so fast he felt light-headed. The lace black bra pushed up her creamy breasts. Another scrap of lace barely covered her woman's softness. Thigh-high black stockings almost had him whimpering.

Kneeling, he rolled one stocking down her long, elegant leg, his teeth and tongue nipping, teasing as he went. By the time he finished removing both, Dianne was sitting on the bed, her body trembling. He stared at her, awed by her beauty. He wanted to be inside her with a consuming urgency.

While he had been gentle with her, he tore off his own clothes until he was naked. She stared at his manhood, then she touched him, her hands stroking. Air hissed though gritted teeth. He was on the edge, knew it. Brushing her hand away, he removed her panties, promising himself that he'd return later, and then her bra. Aware that he was teetering on the edge, he reached into the bedside table and sheathed himself, then kissed her breasts, making his way down her irresistible body until he was kissing the most intimate part of her.

She bucked beneath him, moaned his name. He felt her body moving closer to release, and joined them with one sure thrust. Buried deeply, her legs clamped around him. He pumped into her over and over. She met each thrust willingly.

They shattered together. His breath coming in harsh spurts, he gathered her closely to him and rolled over so she would be on top. He felt at ease for the first time since he'd walked into Dianne's apartment building and seen the shattered look on her face. One arm tightened possessively as the other stroked her from her hips to the nape of her neck.

"Mmmm," she murmured, moving against him as if to get more comfortable.

If she planned to go to sleep on top of him, it would be his pleasure. "Go to sleep. I'm here," he said, kissing her shoulder.

She sighed, sending a rush of warm air across his chest. Her body softened, her heartbeat slowed into a steady rhythm. She was asleep.

Alex kept up the slow, steady sweep of his hand. She was going to be all right, and when she was, he'd tell her how he felt. Gathering her closer, he pulled the covers over them and followed her into sleep.

Chapter 10

After an incredible night in Alex's arms, Dianne had awakened still sprawled on top of him. She had the opportunity to study his face at her leisure. He was heartbreakingly handsome, but he was also kind, gentle, dependable, and fiercely loyal. He deserved the best. She wasn't, but maybe, just maybe she could keep trying until she learned how. Slipping quietly out of bed, she'd showered, dressed, and gone to the kitchen to prepare breakfast.

She'd just finished placing the bacon and eggs on the table when her body sensed Alex was near. She turned, saw the proud look on his face. Then she was in his arms, his mouth kissing her as if he were starving for the taste of her.

"H-have a seat," she managed when he lifted his head. "I'll get your coffee."

"You sit down. I'll get it." Urging her into a chair, he filled both their cups, then took his seat. "I want you to keep the credit card in case you need anything."

"Alex, I can't—"

"Yes, you can." He picked up his toast. "I'd feel better

knowing you have backup if you run out of cash. Which reminds me." He pulled four crisp fifty-dollar bills from his coat pocket. "And before you go all huffy, just keep them in your wallet for emergencies. You can give them back to me once you have a job."

Dianne's stomach knotted. Job. Of course he expected her to work. Fear and embarrassment swept though her. "Modeling is all I know."

His hand gently covered her trembling one. "Then look in that industry for something you'd like. Or take an online course, or enroll in college. Take a few days to decide what you'd like to do. What inspires you."

"All right," she said, withdrawing her hand to reach for her orange juice.

"Don't worry. It will come to you." He kissed her on the cheek. "Finish unpacking. You can use the closets in the other guest bedroom as well. I'll have Arthur bring up the rest of your things. Feel free to move any of my things."

She glanced away. Dianne wanted to be with him, but it was different now.

"What?"

She blew out a breath. "I don't like being dependent on you."

"You think I'd use that to take advantage of you?" he asked.

She was so startled, she was momentarily speechless. The hurt on his face made the words tumble out. "No, of course not. It's that I . . . it was different when I had a job."

"Then keep your things in the guest bedroom if

you'll feel better, but I hope you'll be sleeping in my bed," he said.

Her body reacted predictably. Her nipples tightened, her nerve endings tingled. "I want that, too, but I want to be able to give something to the relationship."

His knuckles brushed down her cheek. "In every relationship there comes a time when one gives more than the other. It balances out. Like last night when you helped out with my clients."

She wanted to argue that it wasn't the same, but knew he wouldn't listen. "You better go or you'll be late."

For a moment he looked as if he might balk, then he glanced at his watch. "Check your jewelry and designer items first to ensure they're all there. You have a list and they're insured, of course."

"Of course," she said, feeling pleased when he smiled proudly down at her. She wasn't completely inept.

"I'll be home no later than six thirty. If you're too busy to cook, just call the office and let me know. I'll stop to pick up something." Hauling her into his arms, he kissed her and then he was gone.

Dianne watched Alex leave and fought down the panic threatening to overwhelm her. She wasn't a failure as her parents had always told her. Like Alex said, she wasn't the first model to be fired. But the company she had been fired from had been started by her grandparents, and was now controlled by her parents.

Stop feeling sorry for yourself, Dianne. Alex believes in you, she reminded herself. *For now hold on to that until you believe in yourself.*

Leaving the kitchen, she went to the guest bed-room where she'd put her luggage. If not for Alex she'd be homeless. She just had to keep thinking about the positive.

Grabbing a suitcase in each hand, she placed them on the bed, then reached for two more until she had all of them open on the bed or on the floor. There was suits and dresses in the bright colors of summer, eve-ning wear.

A specially designed Louis Vuitton case held her jewelry. Unfortunately, like her mother, she loved dia-monds and designer jewelry. Once the D line took off, her grandfather had let her purchase whatever caught her eye. But she'd quickly learned that she could obtain the items for practically nothing by wearing the pieces to special events. That perk, more than any other, al-ways annoyed her mother. It never seemed to matter to her that she had five times as much jewelry as Dianne and was still steadily accumulating.

Dianne picked up an eighteen-carat diamond Piguet watch and fastened it on her arm. Her mother had been practically incensed on seeing the watch, which Dianne had worn to the Academy Awards and then purchased for pennies on the dollar.

Gazing at the watch, she wondered why her mother cared more for the watch than she did her daughter. Aware that if she went down that road, she'd end up miserable and crying, she pushed the unwanted thoughts aside and opened the secret compartment in the bottom. Removing the itemized list of jewelry, she checked the contents and found everything there.

Finished, she placed the jewelry case on top of the dresser and looked at her clothes. The walk-in closet in the bedroom wouldn't hold a fourth of her clothes. Her lingerie would barely fit in the double dresser. She loved soft things against her skin.

She briefly wondered if she had been secretly trying to substitute the feeling for a person. Her grandfather might have loved her, but he gave pats on the arm, not the hugs she desperately wanted and needed. She didn't fault him. It was just his way. She loved and missed him. Like Alex, he believed in her.

The ringing doorbell interrupted her musing. Leaving the bedroom, she went to answer the door. "Yes?"

"Ms. Harrington, we have some of your things. Mr. Stewart sent us."

She momentarily hung her head. Just what she didn't need, more clothes. She unlocked the door, her eyes widening on seeing all the boxes on three luggage carts. "That can't be all mine."

The uniformed man laughed. The two men behind him joined in. "My wife says the same thing about her things."

Dianne wanted to return his smile, but all she could think of was that she had enough clothes for five women and no place to call her own to put them.

"Are you all right?" the man asked, reaching for the cell phone at his waist. "Mr. Stewart said to call him if there was a problem."

"No. No," she quickly said. "Please come in." The last thing she wanted to do was worry Alex or be more of a burden.

The first man stopped just inside the door. "Where should we put them?"

Good question. They wouldn't all fit in the guest bedroom. She was not cluttering up Alex's other guest bedroom. "Please put then by the door of the first bedroom to the right."

The men began unloading the boxes. When they were finished there were twelve, all clearly marked with the contents, from designer handbags to lingerie. The smallest held her toiletries. Overwhelmed, Dianne barely remembered to tip the men with her last ten. "Thank you."

"Thank you," the men said.

"When you want those empty boxes removed, just call downstairs," the man who had spoken told her.

"I will." Trying to smile, she closed the door, turned and looked at the mountain of boxes, and fought not to cry. All she had to show for thirty-two years was boxes of clothes—and what did that say about her? She shoved her fingers though her hair, saw the flash of diamonds, and lowered her arm to stare at the twenty-thousand-dollar watch. Perhaps she had more than she had originally thought. A plan forming, she hurried to the bedroom.

Alex had been tempted to call Dianne several times while he was at work, but he'd remained strong. As much as he wanted her to know he was there for her, she had to learn that she was capable of taking care of herself.

He'd called Jeff, the attendant at the apartment building, and learned that they'd delivered the boxes. Dianne had looked a little surprised seeing them, Jeff added, but said he'd seen the same stunned look on his wife's face a couple of times when she was going though her closets.

"Hi, Alex."

Alex turned in the lobby of the apartment to see Sin. For once he wasn't smiling. "What's the matter?"

"I heard about the dirty deal Dianne got from Boswell. Anything I can do, you know it's done."

"Thanks." Alex's features hardened. "I could really mess up that CEO."

"Me and C. J. would hold your coat," Sin said. "No one messes with our women."

Alex's brow lifted. "I wasn't aware that you and C. J. had women."

Sin grinned. "Figuratively speaking. One of us in love is enough."

"I'd give her the world," Alex said softly.

Sin shuddered, caught Alex's arm, and started toward the elevator. "I like Dianne, but I hope and pray I never fall in love. Too many complications. I'm flying out tomorrow to Dallas."

"How long this time?" Alex stepped onto the elevator.

Sin inserted his key and punched in Alex's floor, then his penthouse suite. "Depends. Talking to guys with the Texas Rangers and Dallas Cowboys. There's a socialite who likes to light up my nights."

Alex shook his head and stepped off the elevator when it stopped on his floor. "One day it's going to happen to you. You're going to love a woman more than you love your freedom."

The smile slid from Sin's face. "Forever isn't for me. I pity the woman who ever believes it is."

The elevator door slid closed. Alex started for his apartment. Sin was probably right, but if he was, there was going to be a hell of a situation. Love was complicated but, to Alex, the rewards were worth it.

He opened the door to his apartment and saw three empty packing boxes. The tension that had nipped at his heels all day eased. Dianne hadn't let her fears immobilize her. She was fighting her demons and moving forward.

"Honey. I'm home," he called, smiling at how naturally the words slipped out. He could easily imagine saying them for a lifetime.

A few steps farther and his smile faded when there was no answer. He checked the guest room and saw a mountain of clothes on her bed. Frowning, he went to his room, found it empty as well, and headed for the kitchen.

A few feet inside the room, he saw the note propped against the espresso machine. He snatched it up.

Don't worry. I'll be back as soon as I can.
    D.

He was only marginally relieved. She was stubborn about taking his money, but a city like New York was no place to be broke. Perhaps she had gone to get takeout or for a walk. He didn't like not knowing she was all right. Tomorrow he was getting her a cell phone.

"Dianne, where are you?"

The words were barely out of his mouth when he heard a noise at the front door. He hurried out of the kitchen. Forgetting that he never opened his door without knowing who was on the other side, he swung it open and saw Dianne with a smile on her face, and two handled bags.

He pulled her into his arms. "I was worried."

"Didn't you see my note?" she asked.

He lifted his head. "I did, and I was still worried."

"Sorry." She gave him a quick kiss, then picked up the bags she had dropped and started for the kitchen. "I have dinner."

Alex slowly followed. She appeared happy. Gone was the frightened woman of this morning, but there was something going on that he couldn't put his finger on.

In the kitchen, instead of helping, he simply watched her as she set the table and transferred the Chinese food onto plates. Opening a bottle of wine she'd pulled from one of the bags, she poured two glasses and handed him one.

"What are we celebrating?" he asked, still trying to figure out why she seemed different.

"I have money," she said. Without taking a sip, she placed the glass on the table, picked up her purse, and pulled out a thick bank envelope with an unsteady hand. "I don't have to be scared anymore."

The words hurt. He had been unsuccessful in allaying her fears. He'd known, of course, but it still hurt hearing her say he wasn't enough.

She must have seen something in his face because she placed the envelope on the table and came to him. "I don't know how to make you understand that, even knowing you were there, I needed to have money of my own. I want to be with you because I want to, not because I don't have a choice."

She was right, of course. He'd been thinking about his feelings instead of about her. His thumb grazed tenderly over her lower lip. She was taking steps to become her own woman. "You want to tell me how?"

She bit her lower lip, sighed. He wasn't sure if she was unsure, embarrassed, or both. "I sold some of my jewelry."

He tenderly brushed her hair from her face. "I hope you drove a hard bargain."

She stopped chewing on her lip. "I did."

"Good."

"I also took some clothes to a resale shop." She frowned and shook her head. "I didn't realize I had so many clothes."

"I think a lot of women would say the same thing."

"Probably." She went to her purse and came back with the money he'd given her and the credit card. "I won't need them now."

Alex, who understood pride, took the money. "Keep the card for emergencies."

"I'm good." She smiled. "It feels wonderful saying that and knowing it's true."

"I'd feel better if you'd keep the card for now," he told her. "You can stick it in your wallet and forget you have it."

"If it will make you feel better." She turned away to finish putting the food on the plates. "Come on, let's eat. There's one more thing we have to discuss."

Alex wasn't sure he wanted to hear it. "Yes?"

She looked up at him then away. "I want to pay rent. I know I can't pay what the guest bedroom is worth, but I'm hoping my cooking and preparing meals will help."

All he could think of was that she wasn't leaving him, but neither was she leaving his bed. "Considering you might start off in the guest bedroom, but end up in my bed, how about fifty dollars a week."

She licked her lips. Desire replaced worry in her beautiful eyes. "I—I can pay two hundred dollars a week."

He shook his head and placed his hands on her waist. "Fifty dollars and that's final. Why don't we seal the deal in said bed?"

Her breath hitched as her gaze moved to his lips. She licked hers again. "A-aren't you hungry?"

"Starving." His mouth found hers.

Saturday morning Alex woke up with a smile and Dianne in his arms. He'd enjoyed turning her nos into breathless yeses. Nothing in life could surpass the sheer pleasure of her coming apart in his arms with his name on her lips. He planned for a lifetime of such moments.

She stirred, murmured his name, and stilled. His

hand swept her hair out of her face. He didn't doubt she was tired. They'd made love most of the night. Around midnight they'd eaten the Chinese food she'd brought home, then made love again. He was insatiable. Thank goodness she was, too.

Life had blindsided her, but she was fighting back. As Catherine had said, Dianne didn't expect him to stick. He'd just have to show her that he wasn't going anyplace. The first thing was breakfast.

Slowly sitting up, he removed her arm from his chest. She stirred and woke up. "Go back to sleep." He kissed her on the cheek. "Considering I let you sleep very little last night, I'm going to cook you breakfast in bed."

She lifted her head and grinned. "Wasn't that the reason I didn't get much sleep?"

Chucking, he pulled her up to him and kissed her again. "True, and I'm making no promises it won't happen again. Today is Saturday and we have all day to just do nothing."

Something flickered in her eyes, then was gone. "If I stayed in bed, I'd just miss you."

He threaded his fingers through her hair. "I'd miss you, too."

She rolled from him to stand naked and playful once again by the bed. "Race you to the shower."

"You're on." Tossing the covers back, he took off after her, catching her just inside the bathroom. "I win," he said and claimed his prize.

Almost thirty minutes later they emerged from the

shower. It took another fifteen minutes to get dressed. Alex was heartened to see that, as the morning progressed, Dianne's smile remained. She insisted he go to the fitness center when he mentioned that he tried to get there at least once a week. He thought she would remain in the apartment, but she'd followed him and been a major distraction while on the treadmill.

He might have been annoyed if the attention she received hadn't helped to prove to Dianne that her CEO was an idiot for firing her. She was beautiful and men noticed.

Finished with his routine, he walked over to her. "My spotter almost dropped the weights looking at you."

She swung toward him, lost her balance, and landed in his arms. "Are you all right?"

"Always better with you in my arms."

"Alex, have mercy on the rest of us," called James, his spotter.

Setting Dianne on her feet, Alex left with her. Minutes later back inside his apartment, he whispered, "I'll give you a head start to the shower."

She looked up at him though a sweep of her lashes. "Either way I win."

"We both win."

You're going to be all right.

Monday morning, Dianne repeated the litany over and over as she searched the want ads for a job. With the weekend over and Alex gone, she couldn't put off the inevitable any longer. She had to find work. The money she had wouldn't last forever. She might enjoy being with Alex, as she'd told him. What she hadn't liked was not having a choice.

Her hands unsteady, she quickly located the want ad for models. She swallowed on seeing the size requirements—no larger than a size 6. There was no mention of age. There didn't have to be. There were models in their thirties or older who did very well, but most had been modeling since they were in their teens or early twenties.

She reached for the cordless phone to call a few models she knew were in New York, then placed her hand in her lap. Their unlisted numbers were on the cell phone that she had turned in. Then she remembered that two of the women she'd been about to call were scheduled to do a photo shoot for *Fashion Insider* magazine in Central Park that afternoon.

The downside was that Sonya was one of the models. Sonya would be gleeful about Dianne being fired, but it couldn't be helped. Before her courage failed, she dressed and left. She'd make Alex proud of her yet.

An hour later, Dianne wasn't so sure of her prediction. Security was extremely tight. The off-duty policeman hired by the fashion magazine didn't care who she was. She wasn't on the list, and she wasn't getting through the barricade.

"If you could please just tell Ms. St. John I'm here, she'll clear me," Dianne told the guard.

The wide-shouldered man rolled his eyes. "Lady, do

you think I have time to keep running back and forth with that line? Besides, like I told you—" He held up the clipboard. "—if your name's not on this list, you don't get past me."

"But—"

"He said no, miss," a female security guard said, then crossed her arms over her thin chest.

Disappointed, Dianne looked past them to see four models in eye-popping colored evening gowns in various poses on the grass, by the trees. She recalled doing similar shoots, becoming tired with the reshoots, the heat, or the cold. What she wouldn't give to have it all back.

"Isn't that Dianne Harrington?"

"I heard she got fired."

Embarrassed, Dianne tucked her head, tightening her grip on her purse. She had to get out of there.

"I want her autograph."

"I'm first."

Amazed that they weren't laughing at her, she turned toward the women just as she heard another cutting voice.

"I don't want her autograph," a high-pitched female voice said. "The man who fired her was right. She's as old as my mother."

"I'd be hiding my face if I were her," another young voice piped in.

Dianne took a step to leave and realized that was what she'd always done when faced with problems. Alex expected more of her and so did she. Her head came up. Her gaze met the surly glare of two teenagers, probably model wannabes, before settling on a well-dressed woman in her early twenties who looked embarrassed. She had a small notebook and pen poised in her hand.

"You're wearing one of Harrington's designs," Dianne said, smiling. "The peach color looks great with your skin color and the slim skirt is flattering."

Obviously pleased, the young woman grinned and approached her. "I had to save for three months to buy this suit, but it's worth it. The D line might not fit my budget, but it does fit my body." She held out the small notebook and pen. "Could I please have your autograph?"

"Certainly." Dianne quickly signed her name. "That's what we wanted in the design, for the wearer to feel comfortable and self-assured."

"I'm not wearing one of your designs, but my sister has several," said her companion, holding out a sheet of paper torn from the other woman's notebook. "She's going to faint when I show this to her."

"Of course." Dianne's practiced gaze swept over the woman, who wore jeans and an oversized shirt, a baseball cap, and boots. "D isn't for everyone. You obviously like expressing yourself with your clothes. Perhaps one day you'll think about a D."

"How can you still recommend their clothes after they fired you?" asked the first woman.

Dianne started. For a brief moment she'd forgotten. She'd been a brand ambassador for too long to stop because they no longer wanted her. "I—I still believe in the company my grandparents started."

"Why did they fire you?" asked the female security guard, unfolding her arms.

Dianne couldn't push the words out. The outspoken teenager had no such difficulty. "The new CEO said she was too old and too fat. Past her prime."

The woman she'd signed the first autograph for shot an angry look at the teenager. It bounced off.

"The CEO must be blind," the male security guard said, his appreciative gaze running over her again.

Dianne's spirits lifted a little. "I'm hoping Cicely, the fashion director for *Fashion Insider* magazine, isn't."

"My sister always wanted to be a model," the female security guard said.

Dianne had heard the same thing thousands of times. "I never appreciated it until it was taken from me. I hope your sister gets her chance."

The slim woman in her early thirties smiled, showing a wide gap in her front teeth. "She's sixty and has ten grandchildren. Her day is long gone."

"Just like mine," Dianne murmured, fighting the stinging in her throat.

The female security guard looked at Dianne a long time, then hooked a thumb over her right shoulder. "We old, fat broads have to stick together. Five minutes or I'm coming after you."

"Thank you." Bending to go under the wooden barricade, Dianne set out in the direction of the main group of people behind the photographer, aware that Cicely would be there giving instructions. She was as well known for the fabulous layouts in her magazines as she was for running a tight ship.

"Hilda, fix Florence's hair and lipstick, then do something with the circles beneath Sonya's eyes. Maud, sultry not bored. Kate, chin up, chest out," Cicely instructed.

While the makeup artist and the models snapped to do as Cicely ordered, Dianne worked her way up to the fashion director of the magazine, who ruled her department and fashion shoots with an iron fist. "Gus, do your thing. I want those pictures to leap off the page."

Without answering, Gus Bear, one of the best in the business, lifted his Canon and began taking pictures. An assistant handed Cicely a bottle of water, but her gaze remained on the women. Dianne knew she was looking for flaws. Dianne couldn't see any in the size 0 to 2 models. The oldest, Sonya, was twenty-four.

"Done," Gus said, handing the camera to a waiting assistant and accepting another.

"Individual shots, ladies, so remain in place," Cicely called out.

"Cicely," Dianne said, when the last model's picture had been taken.

Cicely turned, her black eyes narrowed with annoyance, then she smiled. "D. It's good to see you."

Dianne air-kissed the other woman, briefly taking the small soft hands extended to her. "You're going to have a fabulous spread as usual."

Cicely lifted the bottle of water and took a swallow. "Nothing else is acceptable. What are you doing here?"

Dianne moistened her dry lips; there was no help for

her mouth. "I need a job. I thought you might be able to use me."

Cicely blew out a breath and shook her head of shoulder-length black hair. "You're too well known as the face of Harrington."

"For some jobs perhaps, but a lot of people don't pay any attention to the model," Dianne said, uncaring that desperation coated each word. "I'll take anything."

"I'm sorry, the answer is still no."

"What are you doing here?" Roscoe Lewis asked, stalking up to them. "Let me guess. You want a job." Folding his arms across his chest, he laughed. "This is priceless. You're wasting your time. You should have been nicer to me."

Dianne's eyes chilled. "Not even if I have to beg on the streets." Ignoring the anger on his face, she faced Cicely. "Thank you. Do you mind if I speak with the models?"

"I do," Roscoe said, a smirk on his face.

"I was asking Cicely."

He faced Cicely. "I will withdraw my shoes from the magazine spread."

Cicely casually took another swig of water. "Do you know what they call me?"

Roscoe's bravado faded. Dianne didn't blame him. Cicely was known as the Ice Queen. She was nice, but if you crossed her, run for cover—fast.

"Cicely, you know I was just kidding." He laughed, or at least tried to. "I just didn't want you making a mistake in hiring her."

Cicely's naturally arched brow shot higher on her exquisite face. She was beautiful enough to be a model, but she'd worked her way up to become a respected voice in the fashion industry. "I don't make mistakes in hiring—and if I do, I rectify them immediately," she said, her voice cold.

"I—" Roscoe began; then he swallowed and scowled at Dianne. She folded her arms and smiled into his scared face. He was a well-known shoe designer, but Cicely had clout she didn't mind using to ruin him.

"I'll help you get your foot out of your mouth because I have meetings lined up all afternoon. We both know you're bluffing. You signed a contract and we have very good lawyers who take a dim view of people who don't honor contracts. But the most important thing is there's only one person allowed to be Ice Queen, and that's me."

Dismissing Roscoe, Cicely faced Dianne. "I wish I could use you. You're what a woman should look like." She nodded in the direction of a large white tent. "You'll find the models in there."

"Thank you." Turning, Dianne made her way across the grass, hoping, praying every step of the way.

In less than three minutes, Dianne had the same answer. None of the models had any leads. Their jobs were booked though their agents. After asking for their agent names, and ignoring the smirk on Sonya's face, Dianne left the tent and hurried back to the security checkpoint.

"She hire you?" the female security guard asked.

"No, but I have a lead." Dianne held up the small sheet of paper. "Thank you."

"Good luck."

"Thanks." Dianne hurried away to find a quiet area to call the agencies.

Chapter 11

In took exactly thirty-three minutes for Dianne to be back where she started. The agencies wouldn't even let her attend one of their open calls. She didn't meet the size requirements. It was of no comfort that her age wasn't given as one of the reasons. It seemed no one wanted her.

Slowly, she walked back to Alex's apartment. She needed to save money. Possibly it would help her lose a pound or two.

In his apartment, she went to the guest bedroom and plopped onto the bed. Last week she was employed, having fun tempting Alex.

The phone on the bedside chest rang. Thinking it was Alex, she decided not to answer it. She didn't want to disappoint him again. But wasn't evading him the same?

"Hello."

"Hi, Dianne. It's Summer."

"Alex is at his office," Dianne told her.

"I know. I just got off the phone with him," she said. "I wanted to talk to you."

"Me?" Dianne frowned.

"I know we haven't known each other long, but I wanted you to know that I think you got a dirty deal," she said with heat. "I've had to fire employees, but there's a way to do everything."

Dianne's hand tightened on the phone. "Did—did Alex tell you?"

There was a slight pause. "No. I saw the CEO on a news show. He gave an interview."

It couldn't have been worse. "I see."

"I've left instructions that if he tries to reserve a table the answer will always be no."

"You don't have to do that for me," Dianne said. "I don't like him, but I don't want your business to suffer."

"It won't. I don't want a man who treats people so callously in my restaurant. I had my fill of men like him when I was trying to get the business off the ground," she said. "Too many of them thought I was too young to know what the hell I was talking about. Or they wanted me to sleep with them to obtain a contract."

"I bet you set them straight." Dianne almost smiled.

"With pleasure," Summer said. "I sent each of them the newspaper clipping when Radcliffe's opened and the Who's Who of New York society came, and again when it was featured in *Food and Wine* and *Bon Appétit* magazine six months later. Success is the best revenge."

"I hope one day I'll be able to say the same thing," Dianne said quietly.

"With Alex in your corner, you will. He's a great guy."

"I'm not sure where I would be without him."

"He probably feels the same way about you."

Dianne frowned. "You're mistaken. I've probably complicated his life."

"And made it better. Life without challenges isn't life, my father always said," Summer told her. "You can tuck your tail or bare your teeth and fight for what you want. The Radcliffe clan has never been the tucking-tail type. Gotta go. If you and Alex want to get out for a bite, give me an hour's notice. Bye."

"Bye." Dianne hung up the phone. Summer was successful, but it hadn't been easy. Neither had Catherine's success. As much as Dianne wanted to wallow in self-pity and hide, she wasn't going to find a job moping in the apartment. Getting up, she went to find a phone book. She wasn't giving up.

Alex forced himself to listen to Marco Thomas tell him about the house he and Martha, his wife of thirty years, were building in upstate New York. What was supposed to be their dream home was turning into a construction nightmare.

"The builder kept adding on charges, kept dragging out the completion date. We're more than a hundred thousand dollars over budget and only a quarter of the way finished. We saved and did without for this house." Mr. Thomas looked at his wife sitting beside him. "In the three months Johnson's been building, not one day has passed without an incident.

"I was told you could help us." He grabbed his wife's hand. "At this rate the house will never be finished and we'll be a million dollars over budget."

"Johnson, the builder, said additional expenses are to be expected, but we went by there the other day and wires are hanging everywhere in the basement," his wife said. "Although we paid for particleboard, the label says plain drywall. We're afraid besides gouging us, the house won't pass code when it's finished."

Unfortunately, Alex had heard it all before. "I have a contactor who can inspect the house, but if he finds the house is not up to standards, as you expect, you'll have to make a decision as to how you want to handle the information."

"Why, we want him to fix the house, of course," Mr. Thomas answered as if that were obvious.

"If Johnson is dishonest, he's probably done this before. He could claim he put in the inferior material at your request. Do you have plans and specs listing the items you wanted?" From the uncertain way the couple looked at each other, Alex was almost sure they didn't.

"I can't believe this is happening to us," Mrs. Thomas said, blinking back tears. "We trusted him. We won't have the house or the money."

People who used others pissed the hell out of Alex. Johnson was out for himself, just like the CEO of Harrington. "Let my contact, Spencer Douglas, go out with you as a friend. Say you want to show off your home so his visit won't rouse the builder's suspicions. He's the best in the business. Once we have his report back, we'll go from there. Inferior materials are one thing, not building to code is another."

The couple gripped each other's hands. "Then you'll take our case?"

"No person should be taken advantage of," he said, his thoughts going to Dianne. He could only give her support, not fight her battles for her no matter how much he wanted to. Luke had called that morning. He didn't have anything yet with which Alex could take Boswell down a notch. Until then, if Spencer found the builder was gouging and not building to code, Alex would take great pleasure in putting him out of business. "Yes. I'll take your case."

A week later, Dianne walked out of another employment office. They hadn't been able to help her, either. The woman apologized, but Dianne was too well known as the face of Harrington for other clothing firms to use her. When asked about other modeling jobs, she was told she just "wasn't what they were looking for."

Leaving the office building, she turned and saw Greg Dickerson, the head designer at Harrington's New York office. Her first instinct was to go back into the building so he wouldn't see her. Instead, though, she lifted her head and continued toward him "Hi, Greg."

His head came up. Surprise registered on his thin face. For a split second, he looked as if he wanted to duck into the building himself.

Mild hurt coursed through her. She had always gotten along well with Greg. Unlike René in Paris, Greg was never impatient or demanding with her. "I never thought you would snub me. Sorry if I bothered you."

"Wait," he said, glancing at her then away.

Dianne paused. "What is it?"

He turned to her, pushing up his black designer

sunglasses with his finger. "You just came out of the employment office."

"Yes," she answered. "It appears there's not very much demand for models my size." The words no longer had the power to make her want to tuck her head.

Greg shoved his hand into the pocket of his slacks. "There's even less for designers."

Dianne's eyes rounded. "You too?"

He nodded. "The company needs more vibrancy," he spat.

She touched his arm. "I'm sorry. You're a great women's fashion designer. Grandfather called you one of the best."

Some of the harshness left his face. "Mr. Harrington had faith in his people, made you feel a part of the company. People fear Boswell. Sooner or later, it's going to affect the bottom line."

"As much I want Boswell to fall flat on his face, I don't want him to ruin Harrington," she said. "My grandparents worked too hard."

"He's fired a lot of the people who've been with the company a long time. You aren't by yourself," he said.

Dianne placed her hand on his sagging shoulder. "You're talented. You'll find another job."

"Hope so. I don't want to dip into my retirement fund," he told her. "You're young. You have time to replace yours."

If she had a retirement plan. She didn't. She hadn't given the future a thought until shortly before she was fired. By then it was already too late. "If I hear of anything, I'll call you."

His expression remained solemn. "I'd appreciate it," he said and gave her his phone number. "I'll keep my ears and eyes open for you."

"Thanks." Opening her purse, she put his number inside and gave him her new cell phone number that she'd proudly paid for herself. "Good-bye."

"Good-bye." Greg went into the building.

Dianne stared after him and then started down the street. A block later she paused and gazed into a storefront at the mannequins. Could they all be right? Was she too old and too fat and too well known for this business? She was thirty-two years old and weighed 118 pounds. She might be considered in her prime in any profession except modeling. And no one wanted her.

She wanted to sit down on the sidewalk and bawl. Instead she went inside the department store. It was only a little past twelve. She didn't want to go back to Alex's apartment. It was lonely there without him.

She ended up in the lingerie department. Alex had insisted she keep the American Express card, but she had no intention of buying anything unless it benefited both of them. Fingering the see-though material of a pink negligee, she smiled to herself and wondered if it would count. Probably, if she kept it on for longer than a hot second.

Being loved by Alex was heaven and hell. She wanted to be successful, to be able to meet him on equal terms. Instead she was jobless, practically broke, and without prospects. Releasing the fabric, she started to leave.

"Where are we going to find another model? The

fashion show is scheduled to start in five minutes," said a terse male voice.

"The three models will just have to change faster," came the answer from a woman in a beautiful black suit.

"How is that going to work when three models are supposed to be circulating at all times among the diners and talking to the women about the clothes being available in the store? The Women's Club has had their annual meeting here for years. They shop here. I want to keep them happy customers," the man answered. "I want this problem fixed and I want it fixed now."

The woman the man had spoken to swallowed. "Yes, sir."

Dianne admired the woman's courage and realized this was her opportunity to find her own. With her most charming smile in place, she stepped forward, extending her hand as she did so. "Excuse me, I didn't mean to eavesdrop, but I'm Dianne Harrington. You might have heard I'm available. Not only can I model, I can sell the clothes."

Both of them turned; both gave her a thorough once-over. Relief spread on the woman's face. She grasped Dianne's hand. "You're hired. I'll have Human Resources bring the paperwork. I'm Elaine Sims, head of women's wear, and this is Mr. Ascot, the store's executive. I'll show you where to change."

Dianne happily greeted the other models and the store personnel in the room set aside for the models. From the slightly shocked expressions on their faces, she knew they recognized her name or her face—or both. Thankfully there wasn't time for questions. The store's executive had been correct.

She'd barely settled the black kimono dress over her head before she was on the dining room floor weaving her way through the hundred or so women. That was good, because she didn't have time to get nervous about the reactions of the women or wonder if any of them recognized her. The teenager at the fashion shoot certainly had been dismissively vocal about her, but two other women were also kind. Dianne concentrated on the latter for a brief moment, then thought of Alex and lifted her head.

By the time she'd passed the third table, her shoulders were back, her head high, and she was working the room, smiling as she passed the women. Some were attentive; others were more interested in their cheesecake or conversation.

By the third change, she was actually enjoying herself, glad she was able to answer the women's questions about the color of the fabric or whether the design was right for them. She'd learned a lot about both at Harrington.

"Can I feel that fabric?" one of the diners asked.

"Certainly." Dianne stopped so the middle-aged woman in a yellow silk suit could touch the striped cotton pullover with shoulder detail. "The solid blue cropped drawstring pants are made of cotton and spandex. Besides blue/white, it comes in linen/white and pink/white. Easy wear. Easy care."

"What do you think, Jewel? We're going sailing next week with your father."

The woman seated next to her looked from the woman who had spoken to Dianne and folded her arms. "It's cute and you'd look adorable, Mother," Jewel answered.

The woman frowned. "I meant for you. I like the other two she wore as well."

Jewel affectionally patted her mother's arm. "Thanks for thinking of me, but you know nothing in this store fits me." Her smile a bit wistful she said to Dianne, "Thanks for your time."

"Thank you." Dianne moved on, but she couldn't get what the woman's daughter had said out of her mind. She'd been fretting because she was a ten. She could admit it now, she thought as she took the fourth clothing change, but she could shop in all the major stores. She could even wear some petites.

This time, as Dianne made her way through the table aisles, she made a point to pay more attention to the women, especially those whose figures were fuller. She discovered that most of them barely glanced at her. She even heard a few comments that "they" should have some real women modeling. One voluptuous woman even commented that she could wear the sand-colored linen sleeveless sheath dress—if she bought two of them and sewed them together. She high-fived the woman sitting next to her. The entire table broke into laughter.

Dianne didn't smile as she left the dining room for the final time. She'd been fired because her size didn't fit the image of what Boswell wanted. Some of the women in the dining room might be able to laugh it off that certain fashion lines excluded them, but Dianne couldn't. It was her life.

"Ms. Harrington, you were sensational," Ms. Sims said as Dianne returned to the dressing room. "My card. We have these fashion events once a month. The store would love to have you model again. You'd be a tremendous draw."

Dianne was flattered, and she would have jumped at the chance two hours ago, but now she had other ideas buzzing though her head. "Thank you. You can't imagine how much this meant. Can I call you?"

Disappointment touched the woman's face. "Please do. Your check will be mailed."

"Thank you. While I'm here, I want to do some browsing."

Ms. Sims immediately brightened. "You're in the right store."

Dianne was on a mission. She knew the best stores for women's clothes, the little-known boutiques that were high on the lists of women who demanded the best, and the shops frequented by women on a budget. Her grandfather always said it was as important to know the competition as it was to know your own designs.

She didn't even pause at her own clothing size, but went to the larger sizes—when she could find them. Overall, she wasn't impressed with what she saw. She quickly noticed that the selection grew scarcer, the colors and patterns bolder, as the sizes increased.

By the time she walked out of the last store and

hailed a taxi, she was bubbling with excitement. Finally, she knew what she wanted to do. She couldn't wait to share it with Alex.

Alex shifted the bouquet of flowers and his briefcase to insert his key in the lock. He longed for the sight of Dianne, but he was half afraid that he'd see the defeated look in her face he'd noted each day that week when he came home. It tore at his heart. It was rough on him, but a hundred times rougher on her.

Each day, the smile on her face seemed to be harder and harder to form. Last night, he'd awakened in the middle of the night to find her turned on her side away from him instead of in his arms.

It had taken only a short time for him to become used to her slight weight in his arms while he slept. He wanted her there through eternity, but she wasn't ready to hear that he loved her and wanted to marry her. He knew she cared by the way she looked at him, the way she trembled in his arms when he held her.

She knew he cared and probably thought the sex was a side benefit.

Finally opening the door, he entered, calling her name. "Dianne. I'm home." No answer. Hoping that was a good sign, he dropped off his briefcase in his office, then went to the kitchen to look for a vase.

He opened a cabinet door, and was trying to remember where his mother had stored the vase she said every home needed when he heard the front door open.

"Alex." Excitement, happiness rang in that one word.

"Kitchen," he said, but he was already moving. He saw her ten feet away. She'd never looked more beautiful. Grinning, she closed the distance between them, launching herself into his arms. He caught her. His laughter joined hers.

Her arms around his neck, she grinned up at him. "I finally know what I want to do."

"I always knew you would figure it out," he said simply. "You have the brains and the drive to do or be anything you want." *All you needed was the courage.*

Her hands palmed his face. "Whatever I did in life to have you and Catherine in it, I'm thankful."

He kissed her. He couldn't help it. One day when she valued herself as much as he did, he'd tell her that she was his world. Ending the kiss, he placed her on her feet. "Tell me all about it."

Her eyes still shone. He hoped his kiss had a little to do with it. "I want to bring fashion and style to women who wear size eighteen and up. I got the idea when I was modeling today—"

"You were modeling?"

She laughed again. Opening her handbag, she withdrew a business card. "I overheard the head of women's wear and a store exec talking about needing a model. I offered my services."

"That's my girl." He gave her a brief hug. "And of course you were sensational."

"The head of women's wear certainly thought so, but some of the women there didn't." Her bright smile faded. "The largest size was a fourteen. The women with fuller figures were left out. I heard a couple of jokes about it, but I remembered how I felt when I was let go because I was too fat and too old."

Alex's features hardened. "You're neither."

Her expression pensive, she placed her hand on his chest. "I've finally accepted the hard truth that perhaps I was." She placed her finger on Alex's lips when he opened his mouth to speak. "In some modeling ways I am, but it doesn't mean I'm not without value."

"Damn straight," he said, his hands on her waist pulling her closer.

"But I can go into most stores and find clothes. Many of the women I saw this afternoon couldn't. Realizing that made me stop feeling sorry for myself," she told him. "I did a bit of research afterward and know that I can create clothes that will make women feel confident and fashionable regardless of their size."

"You'll need financing. You want a partner?"

"You want to be a partner?" she asked, her eyes wide.

"A silent one since I know nothing about women's fashion. One thing. We sign a contract. We can agree verbally tonight," he said. "In the morning we can go to my office and I'll draw up a formal contract." He stuck out his hand. "Deal."

She blinked, swallowed. "Deal."

"Seems I was fortuitous." Still holding her hand, he led her into the kitchen. "These are for you."

"They're beautiful." She held the exotic bouquet of tropical flowers to her chest. "Thank you."

"Not as beautiful as you are." His arms circled

her waist again. "I'm really proud of you. Let's go celebrate."

"Where?"

"Anyplace you like," he told her, sure he had a good
idea where she'd want to go.

"All right. Callahan's."

He frowned. He thought she'd want to go to Radcliffe's. "You're sure?"

"Positive. This time I'm walking away the winner at
pool."

"You were always a winner."

"I didn't feel like it until now." Moving away, she
opened a cabinet door, removed a tall vase, and filled it
with water. "It really feels good to know where I'm going, what I want." She began arranging the flowers. "I
can move out of here and get out of your hair. I'll be
my own woman."

Busy arranging the flowers, she didn't see the pain
flash across Alex's face.

Dianne kept throwing anxious glances at Alex. He'd
been quiet on the short walk to Callahan's. She didn't
know what had changed between them. One moment
he'd been happy for her success, the next silent, almost
withdrawn. It couldn't be where they were going; he
loved Callahan's. His best friend owned the bar, and
his other best friend often dropped by. She liked the
loud, friendly bar as well.

It was nice being in a place where you could relax, a
place with friends, good friends. She'd never had that

before. Being with Alex, loving him had given her so much. And this time, if someone asked what she did, she wouldn't embarrass him. She'd be able to say she was a fashion designer.

He reached for the door. She stopped him with a tentative touch on his arm. "We don't have to go."

He looked down at her, but the smile she was so used to seeing was gone. "No. It's what you want."

She stared up into his strong handsome face. He'd always given her what she wanted. To her shame she'd greedily taken.

"Excuse me," a man said behind them.

His mouth tight, Alex released the door handle and stepped aside. "What is it, Dianne?"

"Are you mad at me?"

"Why would I be mad at you?" he asked, raking a hand over his hair.

She might not be a lawyer, but she knew when someone was evading the issue, when he was annoyed. She'd grown up with parents who were both. "I don't know, that's why I'm asking."

He blew out a breath. "Look, Dianne, I've had a long day."

She stuck her hands in her pockets of her slacks, unconsciously hunching her shoulders. "That's what my parents always said when they didn't want to be bothered with me."

"What?"

She glanced away. She knew he'd heard her and she wasn't about to repeat the humiliating statement.

"You're comparing me to *them*?"

The way he spat out *them* put her on guard. She finally looked at him. She'd seen Alex angry, but this was different. In a heartbeat she realized why. She'd hurt him. She quickly closed the distance separating them. "No, never. Never," she repeated, catching his arm when he remained stiff. It was like holding warm steel.

"This is turning out all wrong. I'd planned to come here tonight and let C. J. and the others know I wasn't unemployed, that I was starting a design house." Her hand fell, but she kept her gaze on him. "I didn't want you ashamed of me."

"You think I'm ashamed of you?" he shouted, with no less anger than before. "Where did you get a crazy idea like that? I'd do anything for you."

Her smile wobbled. "Just like always, you're there for me. I wanted you to be proud of me. Show your friends that you weren't dating a loser." She glanced away. "We can leave now."

"I ruined that for you. I'm sorry."

"You have nothing to be sorry for," she told him, meaning it. "Without you, there's no telling where I'd be. My parents certainly don't care. I would have been too ashamed to call Catherine. I had no one until you."

"Then why are you in such a rush to leave?" He took her arms. "To my knowledge, you haven't drawn a single design, yet you're already planning to leave me."

She felt his hands tighten when he said *leave me,* saw his beautiful black eyes darken with misery even in the dim light. He deeply, truly cared about her. For once, she'd done something right. "It wasn't you I wanted to leave, it was my dependence on you. I want to stand on my own feet, support myself the way Catherine does, the way your mother does. That's what I meant. I can't imagine not having you in my life. I'm sorry if you thought otherwise."

"Dianne." He jerked her to him, his mouth finding hers. The kiss was healing and boldly erotic.

"Let's go home," she breathed when she finally lifted her head.

"Not on your life. You're having your moment." Grinning broadly, Alex turned with Dianne to see Summer standing next to Sin by the front door of Callahan's.

Summer sighed and straightened. "Makeup sex would have been better."

"Get lost before you embarrass Dianne," Alex ordered, but he was smiling.

By his side, Dianne grinned and leaned more fully against Alex. "Postponed, not taken off the agenda."

Alex laughed and pulled Dianne to him for a quick kiss; then they simply smiled at each other.

"Alex picked a winner." Sin grinned. "And he managed to pull his foot out of his mouth."

"And they're having makeup sex," Summer murmured.

Sin stared at Summer, a mischievous grin on his devilishly handsome face. "Going through a dry spell?"

Summer's eyes narrowed in her beautiful sculptured face. "Mention what I said in any way, shape, or fashion ever and you'll never get a table at Radcliffe's again." Turning, she went back into the bar.

"Move out of the way, Sin," Alex told him jovially. "We have some celebrating to do."

Sin was already opening the door, searching for Summer.

In the back booth of the bar, Alex, Dianne, and Summer sat on one side, and Sin and C. J. on the other. In front of them was beer for the men and red wine for the women. Alex tapped his longneck with his key ring. "Dianne has an announcement she wants to make."

Dianne smiled, moistened her lips. "It might be a bit early, but I wanted to share with you my new venture, clothing designs for full-figured women. Clothes are more than covering, they tell you about the wearer, give a woman confidence, style. Every woman deserves that."

Summer applauded. "My best friend in college had a hellish time finding clothes that didn't look like shapeless sacks. Most didn't have a good design. When you have your first show, let me know so I can tell her."

"I will." Dianne glanced at Alex. "Alex is going to be my partner."

"Behind-the-scenes partner," Alex rushed to say when Sin and C. J. grinned.

"To Dianne and Alex." Summer lifted her glass. "And boundless success."

"To Dianne and Alex, and boundless success," Sin and C. J. repeated.

"Thank you, all of you," Dianne said, her hands wrapped around her wineglass. "All I have is an idea, but I feel so strongly about it."

"This bar was an idea for my uncle," C. J. said.

"So was Radcliffe's," Summer said, sipping her wine.

"Going with your gut takes courage." Sin picked up

his bottle and tipped the top toward Dianne. "My grand-father always said a lot of people miss tomorrow by looking back at yesterday."

"That's what I was doing, probably would have kept doing if not for Alex," Dianne told then, briefly placing her head on his shoulder.

Summer lifted her glass and sipped. "That's our Alex, steady and strong."

Alex eyed the glass in Summer's hand. "You're being very philosophical after only one glass of wine. Any particular reason?"

"I received my tenth request to be a bridesmaid today." She finished off the glass. "Kara, my top chef."

"So that's why you dropped by here before the evening crowd," C. J. noted.

"I have competent staff," Summer said.

"But you like hands-on," Sin put in.

"Summer's staff is competent. She can take a bit of time off." Dianne placed her hand on the other woman's arm. "Are you up for a game of pool?"

"Let's go," Summer said, placing her glass on the table.

Alex scooted out and stood. "I'll go rack them for you."

"We'll manage," Dianne said and walked away with Summer.

Sin came to his feet, and so did C. J. "It's hard to say which one is the worse player."

C. J. folded his muscled arms across his chest. "That won't matter."

"Summer needs to vent whatever is bothering her,

and cracking a pool ball is better than alcohol." Worried, Alex put his hands on his hips.

"She said something outside . . ." Sin's voice trailed off.

"What?" Alex asked.

"I'll let you know when I figure it out." Hands in the pockets of his slacks, Sin went to the pool area and leaned against the wall to watch the women play.

"Get lost, Sin." Summer racked up the balls.

He didn't move. "With my privileged information, isn't it best if you know where I am?"

Her eyes narrowed. "You always have an answer, don't you?"

"I thought so until a little while ago."

Dianne glanced between the two of them. "Women only."

Sin came to his full height of six foot three. "You know I'll figure it out."

"Until then, you know the way to the bar." Summer chalked her stick and hit the cue ball. Other balls scattered and dropped into the side pocket. When she looked up, Sin was gone.

"You're good. I probably won't give you much of a game." Dianne eyed the ball.

"I'm usually terrible. You gave me the time I needed, and a target to hit." Summer glanced toward the bar.

Dianne's gaze followed. "Better than Sin's head."

"That's debatable," Summer said, her mouth curving into a natural smile.

Dianne powered her cue. "I've never been a bridesmaid, not even close as far as I know."

Summer leaned on her stick. "Believe me, it loses its luster after the third or fourth time. You begin to wonder . . ." Her voice trailed off.

"What's wrong with you?" Dianne finished.

"Alex's right, I'm not the philosophical type. I haven't had time. After I lost my parents, all I could think of was opening the restaurant to carry on their dream." Summer shoved a hand through her long black hair. "My manager just learned today that she's expecting. She and her husband want me to be the baby's godmother."

Dianne looked toward the bar. Alex, on a bar stool, smiled and saluted her with his beer bottle. She blew him a kiss. "Some of us have to wait longer to grab the brass ring, but that just means we'll appreciate it more."

"Alex never dated much. C. J. gets around, but Sin's little black book is probably the size of a phone book." Summer faced away from the bar. "I've spent so much time making the restaurant a success, I wonder if there's room for anything else."

"From the way men practically drool over you, I'd say you have a few more years before we have to put you in a rocking chair." Bending, Dianne hit the cue ball and missed every ball on the table. She straightened and made a face.

"That's just like my life: missing everything and not seeing what was in front of me. Don't be like me or like the people Sin's grandfather talked about. You'll make a great godmother, an attentive bridesmaid, and when your time comes to walk down that aisle as the bride, it will be right because you won't be able to help yourself. Nor will you settle for anything less."

"You love him," Summer said softly.

"With all my heart." Dianne's voice trembled, firmed. "I want to be worthy of him, but first I have to be worthy of myself. That means having the kind of confidence in myself that you have. And please don't tell him."

"I won't."

"Thank you. Now take your shot."

Chapter 12

Dianne woke up the next morning with a definitive plan. First, make love with Alex; second, send him off with a smoldering kiss after breakfast; then get to work on her designs. By nine she was at the kitchen table with a sketch pad she'd picked up from a drugstore on the way back from Callahan's.

She knew what she wanted to begin with: simple lines and soft material, perhaps jersey to drape over the body and cottons for easy care. For colors she wanted a hint of pale blush with a tinge of beige, white, and black.

As she worked on the basics of her designs for most of the day she realized she had the ideas, but she needed help in making them come to life. Tapping the pen on the sketch of an A-line dress, she leaned back in the chair and gazed out the window. Her grandfather had designers who worked by themselves or, when necessary, as a team.

Getting up, she went to her hobo bag in the master bedroom, dumped the contents, and located the slip of paper she'd hastily written Greg Dickerson's phone number on. Taking a seat on the bed, she gazed at the number.

Would he even consider coming to work with her? He'd started with the company after she'd worked with the design team. He'd only seen her as a model. Then, too, if he agreed, they wouldn't be able to pay him his usual salary at first. He'd have to understand that, but perhaps he was willing to take a chance . . . if he hadn't already found a job.

She picked up the phone and dialed. It was answered on the second ring.

"Hello, Greg Dickerson."

Dianne's grip on the cell phone tightened. Too tense to remain seated, she came to her feet. "Hi, Greg. It's Dianne."

"Oh, hi, Dianne."

Some of the enthusiasm left his voice. Dianne understood. He had probably been hoping the call was about a job. "Greg, I want to meet with you about a job opportunity if you're interested."

"A job?" His voice perked up. "You heard something while you were looking?"

"Not exactly." She swallowed and sat back down. "I've decided to start my own fashion design line for women with full figures. I'd like to hire you to be on my design team."

"Who else is on the team?" he asked.

"Just the two of us for now. I have some preliminary sketches I'd like for you to see and we can discuss things further," she said.

"What's the salary?" Greg asked.

Dianne twisted uneasily in her seat. "Why don't we discuss that when you come over for dinner tonight and meet my business partner, Alex Stewart. Say around seven," she told him, giving him the address.

"I'll be there, but I'm not committing to anything," he said.

"I understand. We'll see you at seven. Good-bye, Greg." Dianne disconnected and called Alex. "Mr. Stewart, please. Dianne Harrington calling."

"Certainly, Ms. Harrington. Just a moment."

"Thank you."

"Hi, beautiful."

Dianne went soft inside. "Hi, Alex. I hope I'm not interrupting anything."

"I'm going over some briefs," he said. "How are the sketches going?"

"Great, but I think they need another eye," she told him. "That's what I wanted to talk to you about. The other day while I was out looking for a job, I happened to run into Greg Dickerson, a designer of women's wear. He was a casualty of Theo Boswell as well. I just spoke with him and invited him to dinner tonight to discuss working with me and to meet you. I hope it's all right."

"I told you to consider the place as yours. I'm glad to hear you're making progress, and this time we're having contracts."

Alex was going to make sure that this time Dianne wasn't screwed over. Greg Dickerson was at least sixty, balding, thin as a rail, and no more than five feet tall. "Before you look at Dianne's designs, I'm sure you understand that she'd like you to sign an agreement that you won't design anything similar for at least six months. If you do decide to join Dianne's firm, you'll have to sign a noncompete form for a year."

"I'll sign the agreement about the designs, but I need to see them first to see if there's any promise in them," Greg said, then turned to Dianne sitting next to him at the dining room table after dinner. "I don't want to tie myself up with a firm that's not going anyplace."

"I understand, Greg." Dianne came to her feet. "I'll get the sketches."

Alex watched her leave the room. He knew nothing about fashion design, even less about women's clothes. He'd almost been glad she wanted to wait until Greg was there to show him her sketches. He just hoped and prayed whatever Greg's decision, Dianne wouldn't give up on her dream.

"Here they are." Dianne held the sketches to her chest, then gave the pad to Greg. The designer pushed his tortoiseshell glasses up on his nose and flipped open the cover sheet.

Alex rose from his seat to stand and curve his arm around Dianne's waist. Feeling her tremble, he kissed her forehead and waited.

Greg flipped through the pages, pausing briefly to study each design until he'd seen all seven. "There's not enough for a collection."

"Then you think they have promise?" Dianne asked, moistening her lips.

Greg came to his feet, his gaze direct. "Promise isn't enough in this industry, and you know it as well as I do."

Dianne swallowed the rising fear. "I do, but I also know the industry is always looking for the next big thing." She nodded to the sketch pad in his hand. "There's a tremendous, untapped market for middle-class, full-figured women's clothes and I intend to be the one to bring it to the forefront."

"Again, big words don't cut it in this business."

"Dianne intends to back them up," Alex said. "Her grandfather saw her talent when she helped with the original D line. She knew what young women wanted then, and she knows what women want now."

"How?" Greg asked. "That fool Boswell might have fired you because he said you were overweight, but you're nowhere near full-figured size so you have no personal experience."

"*Fool* is putting it mildly," Alex practically snarled.

Dianne was surprised she didn't feel the need to cry and tuck her head in embarrassment. The reason stood next to her. Alex had shown her she was more than a dress size. She wanted to show other women the same thing.

"I might not be full-figured, but I know what it is to be judged because of your dress size, dismissed, made to feel worthless. From listening to women at the fashion show at the department store, many feel the same way when they walk into a store and can't find their size—or if they do, the construction or design or fit isn't what they're looking for."

"Dianne's clothes will change that." Alex stared down at her, then looked at Greg. "She has the ideas, but she needs someone of your expertise and talent to help her dream come true. Every woman looking for that perfect dress will be able to make that a reality."

Greg grunted. "I can believe you're a lawyer."

"Then you're going to work with me?" Dianne asked.

Greg opened the pad again to the first sketch. "Darts at the waist would make the sheath fit better. I'd do a scoop or square neck, and save the V for after five or evening. Some women might not mind the cleavage, but others might if they're in the work place."

Her heart thumping, Dianne stepped beside him. "I see. What else?"

"If the dress was black, we could pair it with a waterfall cardigan that stopped just below the hips." He took a pen from the inside of his jacket, went to the dining room table, and began to sketch.

Dianne glanced around for a pen and smiled at Alex when he handed her one. "Added to the collection could be a white/black cotton jersey top with black rose graphics on the front and on one shoulder in the back."

Greg nodded as Dianne drew the top in the corner of the page. "She would be set to leave work for a business trip to dress up or down."

"I first thought of white and black, but now I'm thinking yellow. Maybe a cropped cardigan or cargo jacket with a ruffled collar that she could toss in the suitcase or add on the day when the weather was uncertain," Dianne murmured. "Or she needed a punch of color."

"Or just felt sassy," Greg said.

He and Dianne looked at each other and laughed. Slowly they straightened. Dianne's smile faded as Greg's smile disappeared. "You understand what I want to do, you understand design and what women want. I need you."

"If I take you up on your offer, I might miss signing with an established firm," he reasoned.

"But you could also be in the forefront of a new wave of designs for women of all shapes," Dianne cajoled.

"From what I just heard, you and Dianne make a great team." Alex held out the contract. "You'll get credit on all of the designs you do with Dianne."

"I don't want to be tied down," Greg murmured.

"I understand. I'll show you out." Alex tossed the contract on the table. "Thank you for coming, but obviously you aren't right for this position. Dianne needs, deserves someone who is fully committed to the company, not someone waiting for something better to come along."

Greg looked as uncertain as Dianne felt. She might have wanted Alex to try harder to persuade Greg, but she realized he was right. Whoever she hired to work with her as a designer had to be fully committed. "If you hear of anyone else, please ask them to contact me."

"I'll see you out." Alex lightly took Greg's arm and steered the still-silent man toward the front door. "I know I don't have to remind you of the noncompete clause and nondisclosure agreements you signed."

"Grandfather trusted you completely. I know we can also." Dianne stopped by the front door. "Thank you again for coming. Good luck."

"Thank you for coming." Alex opened the door and stuck out his hand. "Good night."

Greg frowned, looked from Alex's hand to Dianne. "I didn't say I didn't want the position."

Excitement rushed through Dianne, but before she could say anything, Alex slipped his hand into his pocket and said, "You didn't say you did, either."

"Lawyers." The way Greg said the word, it wasn't a compliment.

Alex said nothing.

Dianne wanted to ask Greg if he was taking the job, but she would follow Alex's lead. She clamped her teeth together to keep from blurting out the question.

"Close the door. Where's the contract?"

Dianne made a motion to hug Greg, but Alex caught her arm. She and Greg stared at him.

"Only if we have your complete devotion to the firm," Alex said. "Just killing time won't do it."

"I—"

"Greg wouldn't do that." Dianne cut the outraged man off and faced Alex. "I trust him completely."

Alex closed the door and stuck out his hand. "Dianne's faith in you is enough. I trust she won't regret it."

Greg took his hand. "If she does, I guess I'll hear from you."

The handshake was firm. "No guess about it," Alex told him.

Alex was looking out for her again. She wanted to kiss him, then take him to bed. Later. "After we sign the contract, let's have a toast."

Seemingly mollified, Greg followed Dianne to Alex's office. Picking up the contract, she handed him a pen. He signed his name with a flourish.

"I'll get those drinks." Alex moved to the bar in a corner of the office.

Grinning, Dianne stuck out her hand. "Welcome to D and A of New York."

"You were brilliant," Dianne said after Greg had left.

Smiling indulgently, Alex curved his arms around her. "You shouldn't have had that second glass of wine."

She kissed his chin. "I'll have you know I can handle more than a couple of glasses of wine. And great wine it was, too." She backed away, twirled, and came back to him. "I'm just happy." Her smile trembled then firmed. "You made that happen."

"We're partners." He hoped for a lifetime.

"Damn straight." She chuckled, took a deep breath and blew it out. "D and A of New York." She shook her head. "My stomach gets all jittery when I say it."

He kissed her nose. "After fifteen or twenty years the feeling will lessen."

"You are the most amazing man."

He frowned. He wasn't sure why her words bothered him. "I'm just a man."

She shook her head. "There's nothing 'just' about you. You're a true friend."

He knew why her earlier words bothered him. He was still the friend/lover. He stepped away from her. "You probably want to work on your designs, I'll go clean up the kitchen." He turned away from the frown on her face.

In the kitchen, Alex started stacking dishes. He had little regard for the Waterford fine china, crystal, or flatware. They clanked, clicked, and pinged as he dumped the food and began rinsing them. Dianne was giving all she could. It wasn't her fault he loved her and she was grateful.

He just had to be patient and control the fear that one day she'd walk away and leave him. Helping her gain financial independence was risky, but he wouldn't have it any other way. Dianne needed to see her worth, to know she could be successful.

"Alex."

"Yeah," he answered, keeping his back to her, trying to regroup and stop feeling as if, even now, she was slipping away.

"I wanted to ask your opinion on a design."

"Sure." Dependable Alex. Closing the door of the dishwasher, he dried his hands on a paper towel and turned—and forgot to breathe.

Dianne stood in the doorway in a sheer white short top that stopped just below her breasts and bikini panties.

"I know we should concentrate on day and evening wear initially, but I was thinking that every woman needs lingerie." She presented her back to him, glancing provocatively over her shoulder, giving him another air-stealing glimpse of her smooth back, the rounded curves of her hips he recalled too clearly holding as he pumped into her satin heat.

"Well," she prompted, facing him. "Personally, I like the white lace." She touched the little black bows at the hips. "Alex, you aren't helping."

"I—"

"Alex, this is your company, too."

He might have taken exception to her reference to the company if his gaze hadn't been snagged by the dusky nipples pushing against the lace. It was difficult for a man to think when all of his blood was below his waist.

"Alex?"

"You're the most desirable woman I've ever seen."

Her eyes closed.

"What?" He closed the distance between them, pulling her to him. "Are you all right?"

Her head lifted. Her trembling hands rested on his chest. "I thought—I thought you might be thinking of sending me back to the guest bedroom."

"I probably should, but I want every moment I can have with you," he told her. From the way his erection was nudging her, she knew that already.

"Good, because I feel the same way." Her hands went to the buttons of his shirt. "Being in your arms, making love with you is the best part of my day. It's the easiest thing I've ever done." She licked a brown nipple. "The most enjoyable."

"Dianne."

She turned to the other nipple. "No one has ever said my name the way you do, with such need."

He groaned as her hand cupped him. "Honey."

"You probably have no idea how loving you has changed my life. You gave me every dream I ever dreamed." She unbuckled his belt, unhooked his pants. "Tonight I'm going to show you."

With his last fading strength, he caught her hand. "Bed," he managed.

"I can't wait that long."

His heart nearly stopped. She pushed off his shirt, his pants, and his briefs. His erection sprang hungry and free. Her hand cupped him, ran the length of him, over the broad tip. His legs trembled. He plopped into a chair.

She grinned. Actually grinned because she had him holding it together by a thread.

His ragged breath caught as she knelt, her mouth inches from him, and pulled off his shoes and socks. He stared down at her as she stared up at him, and then she lowered her head and took him in her mouth.

He bucked, sucked in air, and grabbed the arms of the chair. He didn't trust himself to touch her. The need pulsing though him was too wild and strong.

She was killing him, driving him closer to the point of no return. She left him and he cried out, then felt her hands sliding down the length of him. Condom. Standing, she straddled him, her mouth fastening to him.

The skimpy wisp of lace was no match for his greedy hands and hard length. With one thrust, he slid into her hot sheath, felt her clench around him. Pleasure shook him, almost taking him over. He resisted. This was for her.

His hands palmed her hips as he thrust into her again and again. He tried, he really did, but somehow control snapped and he lost himself in her white-hot heat. Her back bowed, giving him free access to her taut nipple. He pulled the turgid point into his mouth, suckled, teased, pleased beyond measure.

Sensation rippled though her as she gave herself up

willingly to him. She hadn't known pleasure could be so intense. She had just wanted him to know how much he meant to her without the words. In his fashion, he had given her so much more.

He rocked against her, sending her careening toward completion. Her thoughts splintered as he pumped faster, stroked deeper and quicker. She wanted the sensations to go on, but felt her body tense just as release shook her, wrung a cry from her as he went over with her. His arms tightened, then his hands swept down her damp back as aftershocks shook her.

She felt boneless, sated. Finally she was able to lift her head. She stared into Alex's eyes, a bit dazed, and felt proud. She was good at something.

"You're very pleased with yourself, aren't you?"

"Aren't you?" she asked, feeling as if she could conquer the world as long as this man was by her side.

He grinned, kissed her long and hot and deep. He came to his feet, swayed, clamped his arms tighter around her, and started for the bedroom. "I'll tell you in a couple of hours or maybe in the morning."

"You're looking awfully smug this morning," Sin said.

Alex's grin widened. "Your grandfather was right about not looking back."

Folding his arms, Sin stretched his long legs out in front of him. "Dianne."

"She's the whole package." Alex leaned forward in his chair behind his desk. "But you're not here this early to listen to me. What's up?"

"I want you to promise me something."

Alex leaned forward at Sin's serious tone. "Sure. What is it?"

"Something I prayed I'd never have to consider," he said, then went on to explain.

Less than five minutes later, Alex fought with the sadness, the shock. "I—"

"Promise me," Sin said, cutting him off.

Alex swallowed. "I promise."

Dianne felt energized, ready to meet the world during the days that followed as their designs slowly came to life. The feeling didn't wear off as she and Greg worked at the studio Alex had found for them. Selecting the right fabric had taken time, but the finished products were well worth the effort. She stared at the black sheath on the dress form, the black-and-white jacket, and felt a rush of pride.

She had helped envision this and made it a reality. She threw one arm around Greg and the other around Alex. "We did it."

"You and Greg did it," Alex said.

Dianne bumped him with her hip. "None of that. We're partners. Who found us a place to work, furnishings?"

"It was better than the kitchen table."

They laughed.

"It's a good thing I brought my camera." Alex pulled the small Nikon from his pocket.

Dianne plucked it from his hand. "We'll get someone else to take the picture." Not waiting for an answer, she went into the hallway, spotted a deliveryman, and asked for his assistance. He was only too happy to take the picture.

"Thank you," Dianne said, taking the camera and showing the man out. Closing the door, she looped her arms through Alex's and Greg's. "Gentleman, D and A of New York is open for business."

Chapter 13

It was done. Dianne allowed her proud gaze then her trembling hand to touch each piece—fourteen in all to mix and match, dress up or dress down. The clothes were a great beginning, but they were just that: a beginning. Now came the difficult part.

"We need to find a buyer."

Dianne glanced at Greg, standing beside her. His face reflected the worry she'd tried to keep at bay, but it just circled and kept coming back. "We will. I plan to start calling today while you keep on working on finishing the line."

"You know it won't be easy breaking through," he said, folding his arms.

"The clothes are beautiful. We worked our collective butts off," she said.

"Too bad that doesn't always count."

She knew he was talking about being fired. "We all agree that Boswell is a fool. He made a mistake when he fired us, and we're going to show him."

"Damn straight." He held up his hand and gave Dianne a high five. "I'll get to work. By the time you find a buyer, we'll have sketches and material swatches for the other pieces."

Dianne watched Greg walk away, then she went to the small desk. She'd met a lot of buyers as "The Face." She had contacts. Picking up the phone, she began making calls. First on the list was Janice Olson, women's fashion buyer for an upscale department store.

"Hi, Jan Olson."

"Hello, Jan. It's Dianne Harrington. How are you?"

There was a slight pause. "Fine."

Dianne heard the wariness and noted that Jan, who had once almost fawned over Dianne, hadn't inquired about her. "Great. I'm calling because I've started my own fashion line for full-figured women. The clothes are absolutely beautiful. Greg Dickerson is working with me. I'd love for you to come by the studio and take a look."

"Sorry. We have all we need. Bye."

Dianne's hand flexed on the cell phone. She glanced at the clothes on the rolling rack and punched in another number. She wasn't giving up.

Alex saw it in her face the instant she entered their apartment. The disappointment. The worry. He pulled her into his arms, his hand sweeping from her waist to her shoulders. "Hard day?"

He felt her warm breath on his chest though his shirt. "They won't even consider looking at the collection."

"You and Greg worked so hard."

"I can't believe it was for nothing."

His hand moved beneath her chin to tilt her face upward. "It isn't."

"So why does it feel that way?" She pushed out of his arms and took a seat on the sofa.

"Because you hit a wall." He crouched down in front of her and took her hands. "Catherine has a saying she learned from Luke, but I've heard Summer say the same thing. When life kicks you in the teeth, kick back."

"They've always had their family and money," she said, then straightened. "I didn't mean they haven't worked hard."

"Do you really think that that was all it took, money and family support?"

He could tell she wanted to, and it made him a little sad. "I've had friends who had the same opportunities as I had and didn't do anything with them, while other friends who came from nothing made a success of their lives. Not just financially, but in who they are as people."

"I know Catherine and Summer had to work hard," Dianne said.

"Don't you think they ever heard the word *no*?" he asked.

Dianne waited a bit. "It probably pissed them off and made them more determined."

"Exactly. Sometimes you have to fight for what you want. If people stand in your way, go around, over, or through them."

"You're not going to let me give up, are you?" she asked.

"You aren't going to let yourself give up," he said, placing his mouth inches from hers. "You're just getting your second wind."

She brushed her mouth against his. "I'll say it again, I have good taste."

"I couldn't agree more." His mouth took hers.

The next morning when Macy's opened, Dianne was one of the first customers to enter the store. She headed straight for the executive offices.

She was taking a cue from Alex and from Estée Lauder, who, when she couldn't get Neiman Marcus to carry her scent, purposely dropped a vial of Youth Dew at the store's entrance. Soon the store was inundated with women wanting to buy the fragrance. Dianne was hoping that once Elaine, the head of women's wear, saw the dress, she'd have the store buyer contact her.

Dianne walked up to the receptionist and produced Elaine's card. "Good morning, I'd like to see Ms. Sims please."

The eagle-eyed woman glanced at the card, then at her. Dianne could almost hear the wheels clicking as she tilted her head to one side to study Dianne closer. "Do you have an appointment?"

"No, but I'm willing to wait." Dianne smiled. "I modeled for her and she asked me to contact her again if I was interested."

The middle-aged woman's eyes widened in recognition and awe. "You're Dianne Harrington."

"Yes." Dianne extended her hand.

The woman pressed her hand to her chest before taking Dianne's hand. "I love your clothes. I . . ." She stumbled to a halt as if just remembering Dianne no longer was connected to Harrington House.

"Thank you. Do you think Ms. Sims might have a minute?" Dianne asked.

The woman eyed the garment bag and picked up the phone. "Ms. Sims, Dianne Harrington is here to see you. Yes. Right away.

"She's coming out to meet you."

"Thank you."

The words were barely out of her mouth before Elaine came around a corner, her right hand extended, a wide smile on her face. "Dianne, good morning. It's good to see you."

Dianne shook the woman's hand, hoping her palms were dry. Talking was one thing, executing a plan quite another. "Thank you for seeing me."

"Not at all." Like the receptionist, she eyed the garment bag. "Let's go into my office."

Dianne followed her, nodding to the people who passed, going over again and again what she planned to say. Smiling her thanks, Dianne stepped inside the neat office filled with healthy potted plants; a small bookshelf was filled with fashion books and crystal.

"Please have a seat." Elaine waved Dianne to a chair and went behind her desk. "I hope this means you've decided to model for us. Upper management was very pleased."

"I've come to show you this." Unzipping the garment bag, Dianne pulled out the black sheath with the waterfall cardigan. She'd hoped for interest on Elaine's face, but all she saw was puzzlement.

"The day of the fashion show I talked with and heard women complain about not having a wide selection of clothes for them. I want to change that by creating a line of clothes for women in sizes eighteen and up. This is one of the designs that my design team and I have come up with. We'd be honored if we could have our clothes here."

"Here?" she parroted, sounding almost scandalized. "We don't carry clothes in that size range."

Dianne stepped closer. "And you're missing revenue because of it. There were several women at the fashion show who didn't pay attention to the models because they knew the clothes wouldn't come in their size."

"We have a buyer for women's wear."

"I'd be happy to show him or her the rest of the line. Perhaps we could meet at Radcliffe's for dinner," Dianne coaxed.

The woman had been about to say something, probably a no, then closed her mouth.

Dianne was sure it was the mention of Radcliffe's. "Of course you're included in the invitation."

"You have to realize that all of the floor space is assigned. It's more than just sticking clothes into the area. Please understand that the decision to carry your line is not mine," Elaine explained. "Even if we did carry that size, what you're suggesting is impossible."

"Perhaps if I talked to the buyer or Mr. Ascot. How can I reach him?"

"I'm sorry, we're not allowed to give out that information to customers." Elaine came around the desk. "I'll see you out."

Dismissed again. Dianne started to pull the bag back over the dress, then stopped and looked up at Elaine. "One last chance. I'm leaving here and going to your competitors. When D and A is hot, your CEO isn't going to be happy with you. I've seen him in action."

Uneasiness crossed her face. She bit her lip.

"We could test the waters with this dress. Just to see if there's interest," Dianne said, pressing her point. "Good customer service is necessary to a successful business. Giving them what they want is paramount. Showing innovation would win points with your boss."

"And possibly get me fired. I'm sorry. The answer is still no."

She'd called Dianne's bluff. She could try other stores, but she had a sinking feeling that the answer would be the same. "Can I ask you one last question?"

"Dianne." Impatience radiated in that one word.

"What did you think of the dress?" Dianne asked. "I just want your opinion and then I'm gone."

Elaine looked at Dianne, then the dress. Dianne pushed the guilt button and walked closer to the other woman. "I helped you out. All I'm asking is your opinion. I'm not likely to go to the exec and tell him."

"I like it."

Dianne briefly closed her eyes, then enclosed the

dress in the garment bag. "Thank you, and because you're so nice, when the line is hot, I won't even remind you that your store could have had an exclusive."

"Perhaps you could leave your phone number," Elaine said.

"Delighted." Dianne handed her a business card she'd had made the day after they'd taken the picture.

"Good luck," Elaine said.

"Thanks again, Elaine. For everything." Closing the door behind her, Dianne knew she'd need more than luck.

Her feet hurting and her body bone weary, Dianne let herself into Alex's apartment. She wanted nothing more than to take a long hot soak, then crawl into bed. She couldn't. Alex had said he was bringing guests home for dinner. He was also bringing dinner. Good thing, because she didn't feel like cooking.

Hanging up the D&A dress in the guest bedroom closet, Dianne refused to sink into depression again. It had taken her grandfather three years to make his first sale. Aware that if she sat she might not get up, she took a shower instead of a bath and dressed in the guest bedroom.

Three years. How could anyone keep hitting their head against a wall that long and not give up?

Almost immediately the answer came to her. He had her grandmother.

Dianne might not have been around him too much, but when she was, she'd seen how much they loved and supported each other. Her grandfather had been lost when she died. Dianne going to live with him had saved them both.

"Honey."

Just as Alex had saved her. "Coming." Smiling despite everything, she hurried out of the bedroom, then stopped dead in her tracks when she saw Catherine and Luke Grayson.

"Dianne." Catherine rushed across the room, hugging her.

Dianne hugged her back. She turned her gaze to Alex, feeling heat stain her cheeks. Catherine had to know they were sleeping together, but Dianne wasn't sure how his sister would feel about it.

Catherine straightened, curving her arm around Dianne's stiff shoulder. "You look wonderful. So does Alex. You've been taking good care of each other."

Nothing Catherine could have said would have put Dianne more at ease. "Alex does a better job than I do."

"You make it easy," Alex said. "And speaking of easy. Dinner courtesy of Summer."

Luke chuckled. "I feel as if I'm in Santa Fe. We still stop at Brandon's for takeout all the time."

Dianne took the two large bags. Brandon was Luke's brother. He owned a successful restaurant. His wife's family owned a five-star hotel. All the in-laws and friends were equally successful.

"I'll help." A large bag in her hand, Catherine tossed her handbag on the sofa.

"Why don't we all help?" Luke followed the women into the kitchen.

Alex laughed. "You just don't want to be away from my sister."

"Guilty." In the kitchen, Luke kissed Catherine on the cheek and began pulling out and opening the containers from the bag she held.

"I'll get the plates, honey." Alex took her bags. "You get the place settings."

"That leaves me to grab the wine and sparkling water." Catherine opened the cabinet.

Dianne stared. "I'd say you've done this a time or two."

"See how smart she is." Alex held out the plates as Luke filled them with seared tuna for the women and porterhouse for the men.

In a matter of minutes they were all seated and eating. "What time did you get in?"

"Around nine this morning," Catherine told her. "A colleague was scheduled to speak this afternoon, but he became ill yesterday and asked me to take his place today and tomorrow."

"She felt bad for Rush, but she jumped at the chance to come to New York to see you two." Luke forked in a bite of steak.

"Of course." Catherine put down her fork. "I'm so excited about the new direction your life is taking. I can't wait to see the designs."

Reaching for her wine, Dianne paused. "Unfortunately, no one is interested yet. I took one of the designs to several stores today and always the answer was no."

"You'll succeed." Alex's hand covered hers on the table.

"You certainly will." Catherine picked up her fork. "You're smart, intuitive, and know fashion."

"And beautiful," Alex added.

"What's your next step?" Luke asked.

Dianne stared across the table at Alex's brother-in-law. He'd asked the question she'd been afraid to ask herself. She had absolutely no idea. "I'm keeping my options open."

"Smart idea." Luke picked up his glass of sparkling water. "Cath, you think I should tell Brandon I had a steak in New York that could rival his?"

Catherine shuddered. "Not unless you want to eat frozen dinners for the rest of our married life."

"Brandon is a bit of a fanatic about his restaurant and the food here." Alex picked up his glass of wine. "Although the man can cook."

Luke turned to Dianne again. "It's scary when Brandon is in the same room as the chef for Faith's hotel restaurant and the chef for my sister, Sierra, and her husband, Blade. Only Sierra is brave enough to have them cook for Blade's birthday."

"But she was smart enough to have them prepare different dishes." Catherine smiled over her wineglass.

"I've invited Dianne to come down to Santa Fe for Thanksgiving," Alex said. "She'll see for herself."

"Please come," Catherine said. "You can stay with us."

"What about Hero?" Alex asked, his hand closing over Dianne's in her lap.

"Your pet wolf hybrid?" Dianne asked.

Catherine gave Luke a special smile. "He'll behave if Luke tells him."

"Me? He lets you give him a bath and runs from me when he sees the water hose and tub," Luke told her.

"Because he likes to come inside sometimes while I write and knows he can't unless he's reasonably clean," Catherine said. "Whereas you let him inside when I'm not there."

Luke's lips twitched. "And I thought we were putting one over on you."

"A woman always knows." Catherine chuckled.

Luke reached for her, stopped, shook his head. Picking up his glass, he took a long swallow. "Alex, I suppose you're as busy as usual."

Still holding Dianne's hand, Alex talked in general about his work. It took a few more minutes for Dianne to realize Luke had changed the subject purposefully. Catherine had succeeded in every aspect of her life. Dianne's hand clenched in her lap. Alex held her other hand to convey his support and faith. They were all there for her.

They all had connections and major clout. Alex and Catherine's mother could make a few phone calls and stores would be clamoring for her designs. One of Luke's sisters-in-law was a Tony and Oscar winner. Another was a renowned sculptress. His brother-in-law was a billionaire real estate mogul. They could make this so easy for her.

"Enough shop talk." Catherine leaned forward in her seat. "I want to see your designs."

"All right." Dianne stood, aware that she wasn't

showing much enthusiasm, and led them to the guest bedroom. "The others are at the studio." Unzipping the bag, she pulled the dress out.

"Oh, Dianne. It's gorgeous." Catherine took the hanger. "It's elegant, chic."

"Time to go." Luke left the room, Alex followed.

Catherine briefly glanced at them, then returned her attention to the dress. "Faith would love this."

Another woman with clout, and yet Catherine had made no offer to ask Faith to help her. "I have to sell more than one dress."

"Let's talk." Catherine hung the dress up, took Dianne's hand, and sat on the bed. "Mother isn't here, so we can do this."

"Mrs. Stewart was a stickler about not sitting on the bed once it was made," Dianne remembered.

"You're upset. Scared. Disappointed. You're allowed," Catherine said. "You've had some hard knocks in the past weeks, but you've also had one incredible thing happen to you."

"Alex."

"When doubt and fear are your constant companions, it's comforting to have a man you can trust by your side." Catherine's hands flexed. "If Luke hadn't been there for the darkest period of my life, I might not be here today."

"But at least you weren't broke," Dianne blurted and instantly regretted the outburst. "Catherine, I'm sorry. I didn't mean it."

Catherine squeezed her hands. "I had money, but it didn't comfort me when I thought I was losing my mind. Having Luke in my life did. I understand you're lashing out at me because you're scared and unsure, and probably feel as if your life has spiraled out of control. I felt the same way."

She might have known Catherine would understand, not just because she was a psychologist or because she was her best friend, but because she had been through the same thing. "How did you get through everything?"

"I found a man I could trust, a man who made me stronger and who understood when I was weak," Catherine said softly. "It was a scary process. There came a time I had to face my demons alone. No one was going to ruin my life."

"You're stronger than I am," Dianne admitted softly.

"Bull." Catherine looked angry for the first time. "You're one of the strongest people I know. It took courage to still reach out for love when you'd never been loved. You weren't shown love by your parents, but you always loved them. You never gave up on them. Don't give up on yourself."

Dianne couldn't sleep. Usually after she and Alex made love, she'd drift off to sleep, sated and happy, in his arms.

Not tonight.

With his arms wrapped around her, her upper torso draped across his chest, she listened to his even breathing. The clock on the night chest read 2:17 AM. They'd said good night to Catherine and Luke hours ago. They were staying in the conference hotel because Catherine had an 8:00 AM breakfast meeting and didn't want to disturb Alex and Dianne when she and Luke got up.

Don't give up on yourself.

Catherine's words kept repeating themselves. Dianne didn't have to think very long to accept that that was exactly what she had done, had always done when life became difficult. And each time she had waited for someone, lately Alex, to solve the problem or to fix things.

She had fully expected Alex to "fix" her love life, and now "fix" her faltering career. Neither Catherine nor any of the self-assured, successful women at Sabra's Broadway closing party would expect their husbands to fix things for them.

If Dianne wanted Alec's love and respect, and she did with all her heart, she had to find a way to help herself.

"You all right?" Alex murmured.

Dianne felt his lips brush against her hair. His words were soft, clear. She'd been wrong. He hadn't been asleep after all.

She hesitated. She didn't want him worried about her.

"Honey?"

"Fine." She faked a yawn. "Good night."

" 'Night." Alex's hand swept up and down the naked smoothness of Dianne's back. She wasn't going back to sleep any more than he was. She was scared, worried.

You can do this, honey. Standing back and letting her hit wall after wall was killing him. He wanted to step in, help her. Catherine had convinced him that he couldn't. This time Dianne had to solve her own problems.

If either of them stepped in, she'd continue to think she didn't have it in her to succeed on her own.

And when she did succeed, where would that leave them as a couple? She cared about him, but was it the strong, everlasting kind of love that would bind them together forever? Once the design firm was doing well and she knew she had what it took to be successful, would she be content to stay with him?

She hadn't seemed to mind staying at home with him, but he was unsure if it was due to her not wanting to face people or because she really enjoyed being with him. He wasn't sure how he'd handle her leaving him.

He'd just have to have faith that she was with him because she wanted to be. Only time would tell if he was right.

"I came to a decision about D and A last night," Dianne said and watched as Alex's shoulders tensed beneath the white shirt.

"Yes?"

He'd always been so patient with her. So understanding. "I'm going to try to schedule a press conference this afternoon."

Alex put down his coffee mug and stared across the breakfast table at Dianne. "You haven't wanted to speak with them before."

"Just the thought makes my stomach knot," she admitted.

"Then why now?" he asked.

She clasped her hands on top of the table, her breakfast forgotten. "I need to get the attention of buyers and stores. They aren't interested in our designs, but they might be interested in my thoughts on being fired."

His eyes narrowed with worry. "It won't be easy. Some of the questions will be deliberately cruel to be more sensational."

"It can't be helped." Her hands unclenched. "This interview can give us the kind of exposure D and A needs to get the word out about our company."

Getting up, he came around the table, knelt, and took her trembling hands. "But at what cost?"

"It doesn't matter." She stared down into his dark eyes. "It would help if you were there. I know you're busy."

He didn't hesitate. "What time?"

"Can you be free about two or three?"

"I'll be there," he told her. "I'll see if Catherine and Luke can make it."

"Thank you." She was used to interviews, but it had always been about the company; this time it would be personal. The hurt had dulled, but the thought was still there that she hadn't been good enough.

Pushing to his feet, he kissed her on the cheek. "I'll see you at the press conference. If you need anything or just want to talk strategy, don't hesitate to call."

She nodded. "I won't."

Brushing his hand across her hair, he walked from the room. Dianne didn't move until she heard the front door close. Getting up, she cleaned up the kitchen.

She wasn't sure if she was putting off the calls or

not. She didn't like the spotlight shining on her personal life. Perhaps because it had never been good. Her mother in no way had ever been shy about talking about her weight in public. She'd associated her weight with not measuring up to her mother's standards.

And despite everything, as Catherine had said, Dianne still wanted her parents', especially her beautiful mother's, approval. The kitchen spotless, she phoned Greg at the studio.

"D and A of New York."

Just hearing the company's name bolstered her resolve. "Good morning, Greg."

"I hope you're calling with good news," he said. "I'm almost finished with the rest of the designs."

"Hopefully. Can you round up seven models and have them there by two this afternoon for a press conference?"

"Probably, but why would the press want to cover D and A?"

"Because they also get the opportunity to question the fired spokeswoman for Harrington."

He whistled. "You know it could get ugly?"

"If it happens, it happens, but D and A will also get press," she said.

"You know what?"

He was probably going to tell her that she was crazy. "What?"

"I thought you'd bail and when you did, I wouldn't have to worry about the contract I signed."

Dianne couldn't keep the hurt out of her voice when she replied, "You don't think very much of me."

"My opinion changed a few days after we started working together," he told her. "You worked shoulder-to-shoulder with me, never complained about the long hours or stiff muscles. I'm proud to be on your team. Your grandfather would be proud."

Tears stung her eyes. "Thank you."

"You get those reporters here, and I'll have the models dressed and ready to strut."

"Thank you. Bye." Dianne hung up, took a deep breath and dialed. Luckily, she remembered the number because she often had to call back to do phone interviews.

"Peter Lovett, *Couture Fashion* magazine."

"Hi, Peter. It's Dianne Harrington."

"Dianne, what's the story with your being fired?" he asked without preamble.

"Peter, if you want the whole story be at my studio at two this afternoon." She gave him the address.

"Talk now. I might not be able to make it."

"I'm talking at two. If you can't make it, I'm sure other media will be there. Good-bye, Peter."

Dianne pushed in the next number and ignored the beeps indicating she had a call. Peter would be there. He was too competitive not to be.

"Howard Cruise."

"Hi, Howard, it's Dianne Harrington." Howard was a freelance writer.

"Hey, babe. Heard you were put out to pasture. Any comments?"

Howard was also rude, but he had written for several high-fashion magazines and had a blog followed by industry insiders. "You can hear every juicy detail if you come to my studio this afternoon at two for my press conference." She gave him the address. "Bring your cameraman. Good-bye."

Disconnecting the call, Dianne went through her media list, ignoring the incoming calls. A bit of secrecy would titillate them and get them there. A couple of hours later she stared at one last number, took a breath, and dialed.

"Fashion Insider."

"Cicely St. John. Dianne Harrington calling."

"I'll see if she's available."

Her stomach fluttering, Dianne stood. Cicely was busy, but she was also well respected.

"Hello, Dianne, and the answer is the same."

Since Cicely didn't waste time, neither would Dianne. She quickly told her about the scheduled press conference. "Women's shapes are changing and they deserve to see themselves in fashionable clothes and in magazines."

"That may be, but the majority of my readers want thin. They demand it, and I give them what they want."

Dianne hadn't expected it to be easy. "You've always been an innovator and on the cusp. Just come and look at the line. I need you there."

There was a slight pause. "You know the magazine runs three to five months out."

"I also know you post weekly on your blog of what's hot."

"Your clothes might not make the cut," Cicely said. "I might hate your designs."

"You won't," Dianne said with confidence.

"I'll come if I can. We're looking over the photographs for the next issue," Cicely said.

"Thank you. I hope to see you this afternoon. Bye." Her heart thumping, Dianne hung up. Cicely wasn't the only one who wouldn't hesitate to speak her mind. D&A had to be ready to deliver the goods when they showed up.

Chapter 14

Alex arrived with Luke and Catherine at half past one. He had forced himself not to come any earlier. This was Dianne's show. Opening the door to the design studio, he was disappointed not to see anyone in the twenty or so chairs in the front area. Over a long table by the door was an eighteen-by-twenty-one photo of him, Dianne, and Greg the day the first design was completed.

"Where's Dianne?" Catherine asked.

Closing the door, Alex glanced around for her. "I don't know."

The words had barely left his mouth when she came out of the back room with a small box in her hands. Greg was behind her with bottles of water.

"Hi. You're early."

She looked beautiful and scared in a fitted yellow sheath that showed her gorgeous legs and toned arms. Boswell was dumber than dirt. "We didn't want to miss anything." He saw fear flash across her beautiful face; then it was gone. *That's my girl.*

"Hi, Catherine, Luke," Dianne greeted. "You're just in time to help. Greg thought of Pellegrino with a little tag for D and A, and a media release to be handed out when the press conference is over."

"I knew I was smart to hire you." Alex took the box containing the press release from Dianne.

"Damn straight, and I want a raise when we start working overtime to fill all the orders we're going to have flowing in once word gets out." Greg placed the water on the table.

"You got it." Alex wouldn't even quibble when the time came. Clearly he was in Dianne's corner.

"What can we do to help?" Catherine asked. "Luke is excellent at security."

Greg looked at Luke's six-foot-four frame, his muscular shoulders. "I think a better use would be for him to escort the women models into the room."

Luke's eyes narrowed. Catherine smothered a laugh. "I don't think so," he said very slowly.

"I'll do it," Alex said. "Dianne, where are you going to stand?"

"Anywhere up front should work," Dianne said. "The room isn't that large so I shouldn't have any problems hearing questions or them hearing my answer."

"If they do, use a technique my audience loves. Walk down the aisle, repeat the question, and then answer." Catherine glanced at the seating arrangement. "We can move the rows farther apart so it will be easier getting in and out."

"I'm on it." Luke began rearranging the chairs. Everyone pitched in.

"Catherine, we can do this," Dianne protested, picking up a chair.

"So can I." Catherine placed a chair beside Luke's.

"She's stubborn, but sturdy." Luke grinned and picked up two more chairs.

In a matter of minutes, the chairs were rearranged. Dianne stared at the door. "I feel like I'm waiting for the doors to open for an after-Christmas sale."

"And they always do." Alex curved his arms around her waist.

The door opened and Peter Lovett entered. Beside him, looking annoyed, was Howard Cruise with a cameraman.

"You're on." Releasing her, Alex stepped back. Giving him a smile, Dianne went to meet the men.

"I'll go check on the models." Greg took off.

Through the door came more people. "I don't think she needs it, but I'll go help her get folks seated," Catherine said and walked away.

"Man, I love that woman," Luke murmured.

Alex wasn't surprised by Luke's impassioned statement. "She loves you just as much."

"I'm not sure that's possible," Luke said. "She's my life. The reason I breathe."

"If asked, she'd say the same thing about you." Alex stared at Dianne. "But it almost didn't happen."

Luke folded his arms, his intent gaze on his wife, who was charming everyone she spoke with. "I don't like to even think about the time when she ran from me. Your sister can be stubborn, but I had a backup plan."

Alex turned to Luke. "Because she loved you. How did you know when she loved you?"

Luke finally turned his attention to Alex, then clasped his shoulder. "A lot of things, but what cinched it for me was the way I felt when Catherine looked at me, as if I was her entire world." He glanced at Dianne leading two women to seats. "Listen to your heart and not your fears and you'll know."

"Loving a woman is scary as hell," Alex admitted.

"And when that love is returned, there is no better feeling in the world." Luke glanced over Alex's shoulder and caught Catherine's imploring gaze. "I think we're needed to get people in their seats. For what it's worth, I don't think you have anything to worry about with Dianne. You decided what you're going to do with the information I gave you on Boswell?"

Alex's hands clenched. "There's a good chance if the information is known, he'll be fired. There's a pretty good chance that when that does happen, the board will also try to get Dianne back."

Luke placed his hand on Alex's shoulder. "Yeah, but since I know you, I already know what you're going to do."

"Dianne's happiness will always come first."

"Dianne has proven she's stronger than any of us thought." With a squeeze of his hand, Luke walked away.

Alex slowly followed. His brother-in-law was smart, and as an ex-FBI agent, he read people well. Alex just hoped he had a chance to experience what Luke and Catherine shared. Once what he knew got out, he could very well lose Dianne forever.

* * *

"Thank you for coming," Dianne said, her smile firmly in place. Cicely hadn't come, but others were there. Only two empty seats remained. Alex, Catherine, and Luke were in the front row. Greg stood by the door to the room where the models waited.

"You said you'd talk about being fired," a female reporter for a newspaper blurted out.

"Yeah, what's the nitty-gritty?" Howard Cruise interjected.

"How—"

"Please be patient," Dianne said, cutting Peter Lovett off. "I'll answer all of your questions if you'll just give me a moment."

"Make it quick," Peter said impatiently, glancing at his watch.

Alex came to his feet an instant before Luke. "I believe Ms. Harrington asked you to be patient. If you find you can't comply, I'm sure she'll understand if you have to leave."

A snicker came from the back row. A camera flashed. Peter's mouth flattered into an angry line. His eyes promised retribution.

"Now, that's what I call bodyguards," a woman whispered.

"They could guard my body anytime."

Dianne kept the smile on her face although she wanted to glare at the two women. Catherine had no such restraint.

"Thank you for staying," Alex said smoothly. "You're here because Ms. Harrington values you." Alex took his seat, as did Luke.

Peter sat up a bit straighter. Hopefully Alex's words had appeased him and soothed his wounded pride. Her lawyer was in top form.

"Harrington House was my life until six weeks ago. My identity, my self-worth was tied to Harrington as 'The Face.' It was who I was. I was recognized in the industry, on the A list, I had a good life that I thought would continue.

"I walked into a board meeting with CEO Theo Boswell and my parents fully expecting my life to go on as it had since I was eighteen and launched the D line. I was wrong." She blinked a couple of times, but kept her chin up.

"Instead of a paycheck I was handed a letter of termination by the secretary of the new CEO of Harrington House, a company my late grandfather had founded. Mr. Boswell informed me that I was too fat and too old to continue as The Face. Even though the D line remained profitable, he thought without me it would do better." She swallowed.

"I was shattered. Perhaps more so because my parents agreed with him." Her arms circled her waist. "They wanted what was best for a company that hires hundreds of people, and while I understood their reasoning, it hurt."

The only sound in the room was the click of cameras.

"I walked out of that meeting with little money and a mangled self-esteem. I didn't even have a place to live, because my apartment belonged to Harrington House. One man stepped in to help me, gave me time to move on, and when I didn't, gave me a fast reality check." She sent Alex a special smile.

"Alex Stewart helped me learn to be my own woman, learn that I have value. I might be fat to some people, but Alex thinks I'm pretty hot."

Alex shot to his feet, pumping his fist. "Yeah!"

Smiling, Dianne blew him a kiss. "Since being fired, I've taken a hard look both at my life and at fashion. Both need some adjustments. I love clothes, getting dressed up, looking pretty and desirable. However, for some women, that is a challenge. I want to change that. Alex?"

Alex disappeared into the room with the models. "Ladies and gentlemen, I give you designs by D and A of New York."

One by one, Alex stepped into the room with full-figured models wearing one of their designs. After advancing several feet, he'd return to the room for the next model until all seven were on the floor, looking fabulous and sassy in four-inch heels.

"Two of the models are size eighteen, two size twenty, and three size twenty-two," Dianne told the media as an excited buzz ran through the room. "Alex. Greg. Please join me."

Both men flanked her. She hooked her arms through theirs. "To my right is Alex Stewart, a renowned lawyer, my partner, and my personal ace in the hole. On my right is Greg Dickerson, a man many of you know and respect as a fashion design genius. With Alex's backing and Greg's talent, we were able to create D and A of New York, a company that will, as you see, create stylish, carefree fashions for full-figured women, who deserve to look good and not have to search all over town for beautiful clothes."

"I get that the *D and A* stands for your and Mr. Stewart's first names. Is that the only input you had?" Catherine asked.

"No," Dianne answered, smiling her thanks to Catherine. After Alex had shut down Peter earlier, others might be cautious in asking a question. "Greg and I are the design team. He makes my ideas better. We tend to feed off each other's energy and ideas."

"Who are the buyers?" asked Peter.

"When will the line launch?" Howard wanted to know.

Dianne pulled her arms free and clasped her hands. "Unfortunately, I haven't been able to interest any buyers or stores that feel as we do." She lifted her hand toward the seven models standing on either side of the media.

"Size shouldn't matter, just as gender or age shouldn't matter when judging merit. I might be a bit prejudiced, but the clothes these beautiful women are wearing are smart, sophisticated, and stylish. Don't you think that all women deserve to step out looking their best and not settle because they couldn't find what they were looking for?"

"I certainly do," Catherine said.

"How about the models? Do they agree?" a woman sitting behind Catherine asked.

"What do you say, ladies?" Greg asked.

"It's about time people realized a real woman has hips," commented one.

"Don't forget thighs," added another.

A model wearing an oversized white blouse and slim pants stepped forward and said, "You were called fat and you're clearly not. I *am* fat, and your clothes make me look and feel sexy. You might have to tie me down to get these clothes back."

Everyone laughed. Dianne crossed to the woman and hugged her, then the rest of the models. Cameras flashed. The excited media converged on them.

"Don't forget that raise," Greg whispered to Alex just before he walked over to join her.

Alex smiled. "If any of you can make it, I'd like to buy all of you drinks at Callahan's on Ninety-fifth."

"Does that include the models?" one of them asked.

"Especially the models," Alex said. "There's a limo waiting downstairs for you as soon as you change."

"Don't anyone change until I can get some pictures."

"Cicely," Dianne said, laughing and hugging the beautiful, stylish woman who had spoken. "You came. Thank you."

"I don't ever want to close my mind to fashion." Cicely looked at the models. "You're right about the designs. I'd like to take some pictures, but not here. What's this Callahan's?"

"A bar."

Cicely's eyes lit up. "Perfect."

Alex's and Dianne's gazes met. C. J. was going to have their heads.

Alex sent Dianne, Greg, and Catherine in the limo with the models. He and Luke took a cab so Alex could warn C. J. He'd had no problem with bringing the media and the models because he figured it would just be the usual scene. A photo shoot that would end up in the top fashion blog in the country was another matter. It wouldn't fit his concept of Callahan's being a bar where a man could drown his sorrow, talk sports, and not worry about what he wore. Women were allowed, but not required.

"C. J.," he answered.

"Plans have changed, C. J. The fashion director of a magazine wants to photograph the models wearing Dianne's designs in the bar."

There was a long silence. "What's the name of the magazine?"

"Fashion Insider."

C. J. muttered a curse. "My mother and sister were in that magazine a couple of months back and haven't stopped talking about it."

"I'll owe you for life."

"And don't think I'll let you forget it." The line went dead.

"Well?" Luke asked as Alex disconnected the call.

"He won't toss us out; past that I'm not sure," Alex said, sitting back in his seat.

Dianne was bouncing inside. Greg and the models were chattering away with Cicely. The models weren't shy in talking about the scarcity of calls due to their size, and their thoughts on the fashion industry seeing size six as the cutoff for advertisement, print, and runway shows.

"We're here," Dianne said as the limo pulled up to the curb in front of Callahan's.

Cicely stepped out after Dianne. She didn't look pleased as she viewed the nondescript red-brick building. "I hope it's better inside."

"It is," Dianne said, opening the door. "C. J. has a great place."

"I'll reserve judgment." Cicely entered, her brow arched over dark eyes, followed by her photographer.

"Go with her," Catherine urged. "I'll hold the door for everyone else."

Nodding her thanks, Dianne followed, keeping her worried gaze on Cicely. She was unpredictable and intelligent. She didn't run with the pack, which made her a wild card and one of the most respected voices in fashion. She'd earned her respect. She had an uncanny ability to see possibilities for fantastic photographs in unusual locations. She'd worked with the best.

"Hi, Dianne."

Dianne turned to greet C. J. She let out a small breath, pleased to see he wasn't frowning at being descended upon in his bar. But he wasn't smiling, either. Dianne quickly introduced everyone.

"A bit rustic, but this place has possibilities," Cicely mused after the introductions were completed.

C. J.'s eyes narrowed. "Possibilities. It's the best bar in the city."

Cicely's brow arched sharply. "You don't get out much, do you?"

Eyes narrowed, C. J. stepped into her space. "You must not, either. A bar is more than a place to swig beer.

Never mind the history of the place, the original wood from an eighteenth-century pub in London along with the railing. The floor is stained concrete so it takes whatever customers dish out, the lighting is old-world, and the bar is stocked with the best beer and liquor."

"And if I want a cosmopolitan?" Cicely asked.

"Down the street. We make real drinks."

Cicely glanced around. "Real drinks for the knuckle-dragging men."

"Now, see here—"

"Clarence."

C. J. froze like a deer in headlights, his head coming up, his eyes no less hard. Dianne turned to see an attractive woman in her midsixties in a white Versace suit that Dianne had longed for, but had felt she'd be unfaithful to Harrington for purchasing. The woman exuded elegance and wealth. She didn't stop until she was standing between C. J. and Cicely, a small hand on both of their arms.

"Clarence, Cicely," the woman greeted. "I couldn't believe it when Alex called. I was shopping, but I had my driver bring me right over."

"Clarence?" Cicely said, her tongue stuck in her cheek.

C. J. looked as if he wanted to explode. "Mother—"

"I forgot," the woman quickly said, then spoke to Cicely in an aside. "He's never liked his name nor forgiven us."

"Mother, this is not the time or place," C. J. told her.

His mother appeared a bit intimidated. "Whatever you say. I just wanted the chance to thank Cicely again. It was such an honor."

"Well deserved," Cicely said, then looked at C. J. "I call them as I see them."

"You—"

"C. J.," Alex interrupted, catching his friend's arm. "Why don't we get out of the way and let Cicely take her pictures." C. J. resisted. He glared at Cicely.

Folding her arms, she smiled sweetly at him. "You have a problem with my guy shooting here?"

Dianne bit her lip, but kept quiet. It was C. J.'s call.

"Of course not," his mother said. "You'd put his place on the map."

C. J. shot his mother an annoyed look. She frowned at him in total bewilderment. "I like flying below the radar," he said by way of explanation. He cut a glance at Alex's hand on his arm, then at Dianne, and shook his head. "It wouldn't bother me if you forgot to mention the name of the place."

"Fair enough." Cicely's arms came to her sides. "I'll leave your man-cave just as it I found it. Mrs. Callahan, thank you for stopping by. As always, you're the epitome of style and elegance."

Mrs. Callahan smiled her pleasure. "Thank you."

Cicely faced Dianne. "Let's get this done."

Dianne was only too happy to move away. As she did so, she glanced over her shoulder and mouthed *Thank you* to C. J. He didn't notice. His hard gaze was on Cicely.

Less than thirty minutes later, Cicely and her photographer were preparing to leave. She'd enlisted the all-too-willing help of several of the men in the bar to pose with the models. Alex watched C. J., who watched Cicely. His easygoing friend was royally ticked. No one maligned his bar. If he hadn't liked Dianne, he would have kicked them all out. He didn't mince words.

His mother left shortly after she arrived. She'd finally understood that C. J. wasn't pleased with any of them, and to stay wouldn't help the family cause of getting him into the CEO's seat. His family had always tended to walk easy around C. J., and even more so now. He held their livelihood and the fate of the company that had been in the family three generations in his unpredictable hands.

They didn't understand what Alex, Sin, and Summer already knew—C. J. couldn't be pushed, and despite his doing everything that might indicate differently, he valued and loved his family, and respected what they had accomplished. He'd run the company, but he wasn't going to do it until he absolutely had to. He realized, like his father and his brother, that once he took that seat at his father's desk, his life would be irrevocably changed. His carefree days would disappear.

"Thanks." With his back against the bar, Alex sipped his tonic water. "Anytime you want to collect, let me know."

Arms folded, one ankle crossed over the other, C. J. watched Cicely as Dianne and Greg walked them to the door. "That was one annoying woman." Unfolding his arms, C. J. went behind the bar to draw a beer on tap.

"Is that why you weren't able to take your eyes off her?" Alex slung a leg over a stool.

C. J. plopped the beer in front of Alex. "The package might be nice, but not the attitude."

Alex picked up his beer and sipped. C. J. liked his women uncomplicated. "This means a lot to Dianne."

C. J. braced his arms on the bar and shook his dark head. "You are such a goner."

"She's the one and only," Alex confessed. There was no sense in denying the truth.

"I'd try to talk some sense into your head, but I can see it's too late," C. J. grunted. "At least she doesn't giggle, and she has the good sense to like my bar."

"I *love* your bar," Dianne said, coming up to them to curve her arms around Alex's neck, then kissing him on the cheek. "Thank you, C. J. Cicely plans to put the pictures up tonight on her blog. Her site gets thousands of hits."

Alex came off the bar stool, his arm curving around Dianne. "Then we better get home and get the computer ready. I'll tell the press to order their last drink, and get Luke and Catherine out of the pool room."

"Greg is taking the models back to the studio to change, and then heading straight home," Dianne told him. "All of us are anxious to see the pictures and read what Cicely has to say."

"Figures she'd have a blog," C. J. said. "She likes expressing her opinion. What the name of the site?"

Dianne hesitated. *"Fashionista Diva in the House."*

"Figures."

Chapter 15

As soon as they'd reached his apartment, Alex had gone straight to his office and booted up his computer. In seconds they were on Cicely's blog site. Previous covers of *Fashion Insider* flashed on the screen. The outfits ranged from outlandish to stunning, but all had something in common.

"All of the models are thin," Dianne murmured.

Alex caught her unsteady hand. "She liked the clothes."

Dianne nodded. "I know, but . . ."

"No buts." Alex came to his feet. "Let's go get our share of the pizza before Luke and Catherine eat it all up."

She was shaking her head before he finished. She slid into the seat he'd vacated. "I'm too nervous to eat."

He swiveled the chair around so she faced him. "Give her time."

"She really liked the clothes, didn't she?" Dianne said, as if seeking reassurance.

Taking her hands, he pulled her upright. "She really

did, and so will buyers and department stores. You and Greg will be knee-deep in orders."

"And I can begin to pay you back," she said, nibbling on her lower lip.

A frown flashed across his face. "Don't worry about that."

"No," she said adamantly. "I'm going to carry my responsibility on this. I want to know I contributed to the success of D and A." She glanced back at the computer screen, then gasped. "She posted! She posted!"

Grabbing Alex's hand, Dianne took a seat.

"Luke. Catherine!" Alex yelled. "The blog is up."

Her voice trembling, Dianne began to read the post.

I had the privilege this afternoon to be among the first to greet a new fashion design house that will quickly makes its mark in the industry.

Dianne swallowed, her hand trembling even more.

D&A of New York will cater to women the fashion industry sometimes chooses to ignore. D&A decided to change that in a fabulous way by creating designs for women of substance who demand style and quality. From the photographs, you can see that onetime top model Dianne Harrington and her partner, Alex Stewart, along with the artistic genius and flair of Greg Dickerson, have created clothes women of all sizes will love. But alas, these fabulous designs only come in sizes 18 to 22 for the moment. Seeing the fantastic models this afternoon reaffirmed my long-held opinion that a woman wearing the right clothes will look fabulous no matter what she weighs or where she is. Enjoy.

"Told you." Alex pulled Dianne to her feet and hugged her; then it was Catherine's and Luke's turn.

"Do you think it would be appropriate if I blog and thank her?" Dianne asked.

"Good manners are always appropriate," Catherine said. "Once you're finished I'm going to leave a comment. I sent the women in the family the blog site so they'll probably comment as well."

"There's already a comment," Alex said, then read.

It's about time. Where can I purchase?

They watched as more comments appeared.

Dianne reached for the phone and dialed. Greg answered on the first ring. "Greg, she loved us!"

"Count yourself lucky that you had the smarts to hire an artistic genius with flair," Greg said with just the right amount of hauteur, then he laughed aloud.

Dianne laughed with him. "I do. I'll see you at the studio in the morning. 'Night." She hung up the phone. It rang almost immediately.

She picked up the receiver. "Hello."

"Where's Alex?"

Her smile quickly faded. She looked at Alex.

"What is it?" Alex stepped closer.

She put her hand over the speaker. "I don't think

everyone is happy with Cicely," she said, removing her hand and speaking into the receiver. "C. J.—" she began, but Alex took the phone from her.

"Lay it on me," Alex said.

"I want to sue for defamation and slander," C. J. spat.

If it had been anyone else, Alex would have laughed. "She didn't say anything directly about the bar."

"The hell she didn't," C. J. flared. "Didn't you read the crack about a woman looking good no matter where she was."

"I did, but she didn't say Callahan's. Besides if you decided to take legal action, the press would become involved and the notoriety you've always avoided will happen," Alex pointed out.

"You mean I have to let her get away with slamming my bar?"

"She didn't slam your bar."

Dianne took the phone. "I'm sorry, C. J. You were trying to help us."

"Not your fault. It's hers. One day she's going to regret her mistake. 'Night."

Dianne replaced the phone. "He hung up. I'm sorry C. J.'s upset."

"He'll get over it. While you were talking, more comments came in." Alex guided her into his chair. "People are asking about the designer. You're on."

Two hours later, Dianne was still on the computer. She'd only gotten up long enough to hug Catherine and Luke good-bye, and eat a couple of bites of pizza because Alex insisted. The response was overwhelming.

"Your designs hit a nerve," Alex said from beside her. "Women don't want to be thought less of because they have a different body shape. Nor should they be."

Dianne shook her head. "If I hadn't been fired, I never would have thought of them."

Alex touched her arm. "Don't sell yourself short. You could have shrugged off the women's comments at the luncheon and just thought about yourself. You didn't. You cared, and you did something about it."

"With your help."

His fingers squeezed. "We're partners."

Warmth rushed though her. "Without you—"

He pressed his index fingers against her lips. She suppressed the urge to bite, then pull him down onto the floor. "You did this. Never forget."

He was her strength, but she was finally coming to realize that he wanted her to believe in herself just as much. If she wanted a future with him she had to be her own woman, and that meant facing her insecurities. "I think I want to start a blog and invite the readers here to join me and comment."

"Sounds good. What are you going to call it?"

She smiled. *"Fired for being too old and too fat."*

During the days that followed, the hits on Dianne's blog grew. She knew such popularity would never have happened without Cicely's post being the gateway to thousands of women. Women were outraged on her behalf. She wasn't surprised to learn that other women had suffered discrimination on their jobs due to age or weight. They became TFTO, the too-fat, too-old crowd.

Hearing other stories, she realized how blessed and fortunate she was to be able to channel her firing into something positive.

And it was all because of the man who held her in his arms each night when she fell asleep. Alex was her strength. No longer did she feel insecure or get that sinking feeling in the pit of her stomach when she talked about the reasons behind her firing. She was quickly learning that it was the best thing that could have happened to her.

She'd even received a call from the AFL-CIO about representing her in a lawsuit again Harrington for discrimination. She'd refused. That night over a dinner they'd both prepared because they'd both gotten home late, she'd told Alex about the call and asked him why he hadn't suggested the lawsuit.

His gaze hadn't wavered. "Because you weren't strong enough to go against Harrington or your parents."

"And now?" she asked, unaware that she was holding her breath.

"Say the word, and I'll make them pay for every tear you shed," he told her, his eyes cold.

Her lips trembled. "Alex." Getting up, she rounded the table. He met her, holding her tightly to him.

"No one is ever going to hurt you again."

She lifted her head. "Yes, they will, but as long as I have you, I'll be all right."

His gaze flared hot. His mouth took hers, his tongue tasting and tangling with hers. Picking her up, he started for the bedroom. "Dinner is going to be late."

She bit his earlobe. "I'll just make a feast of you."

With a throaty growl, he tumbled them into his bed, his body covering her, letting her feel his desire. He touched her and her body went up in flames. She wanted, needed this joining of body and heart and soul with this man. As he brought them together with one sure thrust, she clamped around him. The loving was fast and hard and when it was over and her body spent, she held him tightly and realized something else: She needed his heart as well.

Dianne was working on a design in the studio when the phone rang. Her lip pulled between her teeth in concentration, she ignored the call. She and Greg had agreed they needed twenty pieces to launch the D&A collection. She was working on a dress with a coat, trying to decide if she wanted it reversible.

Reluctantly, Dianne straightened. The phone was probably equal distance between them, but since Greg was sewing up one of their designs, Dianne eased off the stool and went to pick up. "D and A of New York," she answered, again thinking they needed a slogan.

"Dianne Harrington?" asked the crisp voice.

She straightened. "Yes."

"This is Simone Davis, the women's fashion buyer for Merrill Department Stores. I wanted to see your designs, if possible."

Dianne pressed a trembling hand to her stomach. Merrill, a high-end department store, had outlets scattered across the country. Their flagship store was on Madison Avenue. They'd carried Harrington clothes for five years. "That could be arranged. What time would be convenient?" she said calmly, as if her heart weren't doing backflips.

"This afternoon at two all right?"

"You're in luck. We have an opening." Dianne gave the buyer the address.

"We'll see you then. Good-bye."

"Good-bye."

Dianne hung up and squealed. Greg started. Grinning she ran to him and kissed him loudly on the cheek. "A buyer from Merrill is coming at two."

"Well, hot damn!"

"I'm going to the corner deli and see if they have a small tray and a bottle of wine," She said. The phone rang again just as she picked up her purse. Her gaze met Greg's. In his eyes, she saw the same worry. What if the buyer was calling back to cancel?

"No," Dianne said as if to reassure them both. Crossing the room, she answered the phone. "D and A of New York."

"Dianne Harrington, please. This is Steve Miller, the women's fashion buyer for Dawson's."

Dianne mouthed *Another buyer* to Greg. She knew Steve and had had dinner with him and his wife. "This is Dianne, Steve."

"Dianne, I thought that was you," he said. "We're getting a lot of requests for your clothes. I'd like to see the line."

"We're booked today, how about tomorrow?" she asked.

"I'll take the earliest you have for tomorrow."

"For you, Steve, I'll be here at nine." She gave him the address.

"I'll be there."

The buyers not only came, they purchased the spring D&A line. Dianne asked for and was granted a special night to introduce the clothes in each flagship store. With each order, she blogged the news. She received calls from the buyers, thanking her for the mention. Customers were already asking when the clothes would be available. Hearing this, Dianne started a countdown on her blog. At the end of two weeks, they had orders from ten chain stores and two boutiques.

They were going to make it. Dianne made duplicate copies of each order and took them home with her to place in a folder. If she ever thought she was dreaming, she could look at them.

She was only too happy, and so were the stores that had purchased the line, to let the people on her blog know where they could purchase the clothes for spring. Now having the studio made perfect sense. The business offices would be on the top floor, and the manufacturing end and storage on the main floor.

Her life was turning around. She was headed toward being the independent woman she had always wanted to be. Fashion magazines were calling for interviews. She couldn't have been busier, and she enjoyed every moment.

A surprise call was Elaine at Macy's. She wanted to know if D&A would like to show a couple of designs at an upcoming luncheon. Dianne jumped at the chance. If the clothes were a hit, the buyer might order.

She blogged about the event. To her amazed delight, when she and the models climbed out of the limo—Alex's idea—women were waiting for them. It had been Dianne's idea for her models to wear the clothes there. That way women not at the fashion show would see them. It proved to be a bit of marketing genius.

Since there were so many women, the local TV station sent a reporter with a camera. Dianne repeated the story of why she was fired, which propelled her to a new career. When the news story ran that night, her blog hits went through the roof. More women were incensed on her behalf.

"I never would have believed this," she said to Alex as she typed a post.

"Told you."

She threw him a quick grin, finished typing, and hit SEND. "This feels good."

Warm lips pressed against the back of her neck. "I couldn't agree more."

"Hmmm." She momentarily leaned back against him, then straightened. "Don't tempt me. I have to answer these posts."

"It's almost ten. That will take most of the night," Alex protested.

"I'm sorry," she said, typing again. "I want the women posting to know I care. But you go on to bed."

"I want you with me," he protested.

Her hands paused. She looked at him. Desire stared

back at her. She felt the familiar tingling sensation in her body. Her nipples tightened beneath her blouse. She wanted to lean into him, but she didn't want to risk offending anyone. Helping the company be successful would put her on an even keel with Alex, and she could finally tell him she loved him.

He straightened. "Don't stay up too long."

"I won't," she murmured, watching him walk away, wanting to follow him. Firmly she turned, giving her attention to the blog. This was for both of them. She'd make it up to him when she went to bed.

Stopping at the door of his office, Alex stared at Dianne. Was he losing her already? The more successful her company became, the less time they spent together. They saw each other at breakfast, but she didn't get home some nights until ten, and then she'd go to the computer to answer the blog comments. He wanted her to be her own woman, but he hadn't taken into consideration that the more successful she was, the less she'd need him.

Still, he wouldn't change a thing. He wanted her to be happy, wanted to see a smile on her beautiful face instead of worry and defeat. He should have remembered that her life was very different from his.

He turned to go to his room just as the doorbell rang. He was almost grateful for the interruption of his thoughts. He'd find a way to bind Dianne to him. "Are you expecting anyone?"

"No," she said, continuing to type.

Alex went to the door and opened it, and wanted to slam it shut when he saw Dianne's parents. Two beautiful people as cold as the diamonds in her mother's ears.

"Hello, Alex," her father greeted, as if it had been ten minutes instead of ten years since they'd spoken. "We've come to see Dianne."

"Why?" he asked, still blocking their entrance by holding the door.

Her mother frowned. "That should be obvious. She's our daughter."

"When it's convenient. You're not hurting her again."

Her father's smile slid from his handsome face. "We want to see Dianne."

"You're not hurting her again," Alex repeated. "Leave or I'll call security."

"You can't threaten—"

"Mom. Dad."

Alex jerked around to see Dianne a few feet behind him. When he did, her parents rushed past him, enveloping Dianne in a hug.

"Sweetheart," her mother cooed.

"Precious," her father said.

Alex wanted to toss both of them out. Instead he closed the door. Her parents had never wanted or loved Dianne. From the way she clung to them, the hope shining in her eyes, she'd forgotten they'd turned their back on her. Alex hadn't, and he never would.

"How did you find me?" she asked.

"The security man at your old place still had Alex's card," her mother answered, brushing her hand affectionately over Dianne's head. She looked at Alex with a smile on her face, but her eyes were cold. "Thank you for taking care of Dianne, but that won't be necessary any longer."

"What do you two want?" Alex asked, afraid he already knew.

With his arm around Dianne's shoulder, her father stared down into her face. "Our daughter, of course. She's proven she can take Harrington to the next level, just as her mother and I always knew."

Alex wasn't buying the crap, but from the look on Dianne's face, she believed them. "You have a strange way of showing your support. When she needed you the most, you turned your back on her."

Her mother faced Dianne. "Forgive us. It was a calculated risk to push you into becoming the woman we always knew you could be."

Dianne shook her head. "I don't understand."

"Boswell was never our choice as CEO. He just needed enough rope to hang himself," her father said. "Since your unwarranted firing, the board has been inundated with e-mails calling for his resignation. Harrington's public image has taken a hit and with it, orders were canceled."

"Boswell is being replaced, as well he should be," her mother said. "The board wants you back. So do we."

"She's not going," Alex said.

Her father cut Alex a look. "We appreciate your helping Dianne, but you have no say in what she does."

"Dianne and I are partners, that gives me a right," Alex told him.

"Surely her welfare is more important than a partnership," her mother put in. "Harrington House is established. You can't say that about this new venture. The public might be interested now, but what about months from now? Dianne is aware of all the lines that start and then fold."

"Harrington House has established itself as a leader in the fashion industry. You could lose the money you've invested in a season," her father said.

"That won't happen. Dianne will see that it won't," Alex said, wanting to pull Dianne away from her manipulative parents. They were giving her what she'd always wanted, their love and faith in her.

"Dianne, you know how your grandfather loved the company and wanted it to flourish. You can help that happen," her father said. "Come back to Harrington House."

"You want me back?"

"Yes, sweetheart." Her mother brushed her hair back. "With our ruling percentage, you can design or model, whatever you want."

Dianne's stomach was jumping, her emotions all over the place. Her parents wanted her to come back to Harrington. They wanted her. Her gaze went to Alex, strong, steady. "I already have a design house."

"You can incorporate it into Harrington," her mother quickly said. "You can become the head designer of D and A, and continue as the lead model for the D line. You can have it all."

And there would be no place for him, Alex thought.

"What about the other model?" Dianne asked.

Her mother rolled her eyes. "Turns out she was Boswell's niece. The board wasn't happy to learn about it, either. Your apartment is waiting for you. I spent the day having the place cleaned. It's just as if you never left." Her mother reached into her handbag and pulled out a key. "Here you go. We can go there tonight if you wish to see if everything is the way you want. Your things can be sent tomorrow. I can help you unpack."

"You'd help?"

She laughed and hugged Dianne. Dianne was almost as stunned by the statement as the hug. Her mother didn't even unpack her own clothes. She wasn't the hugging type—at least not with Dianne.

"It's just my way of letting you know how proud of you we are," her mother said. "But tonight, we want you to come back to our hotel suite. We want to start making it up to you for all you're gone though."

"Dianne is staying here, and she's continuing with D and A," Alex said. "You turned your backs on her, and now you want her to help the company out."

"We want our daughter," her mother insisted, then turned to Dianne. "Why don't you grab enough for tonight and we'll be on our way."

"I said she's not going anyplace," Alex said.

"That's my daughter's decision," her father said, smiling down at Dianne.

Her parents wanted her. She'd hoped and prayed for so long. It had finally happened.

"Come on, Dianne. Let's get your things, and we

can be on our way." Her mother took Dianne's arm. "Which way?"

Dianne looked at Alex, the one person who she had always counted on. He'd offered hope when she felt hopeless. And she could read absolutely nothing on his face.

"Dianne, let's go," her mother urged. "Your life isn't here. You'll be the toast of the fashion world. You'll make your grandfather and us proud. This is what you were destined to do, and you know it."

Still she stared at the man she had counted on since she was five years old. Not once had he let her down. "Alex?"

"I want you to stay, but it's your decision."

She swallowed the sudden lump in her throat. That wasn't the answer she wanted to hear. They might have started out as friends turned lovers because of her suggestion, but she wanted so much more. She wanted his love, his children. She should have remembered that people didn't stick around for the long haul in her life. She couldn't blame Alex. He'd want a woman who was his equal.

She'd made strides, but her mother was right. Orders for the D&A line didn't mean automatic success. They could be out of business in less than a year. She didn't think she could bear Alex seeing her fail again, especially when he'd bankrolled the company.

"It's this way." She turned toward the guest bedroom, fighting the growing lump in her throat. Silently, she picked up her small suitcase and threw a few things inside, all the time fighting tears and misery.

"I personally picked out several outfits, so you don't need much," her mother said as she grabbed a shoe bag.

Dianne stared at her mother putting shoes into the bag, then going to her jewelry case and picking it up. Dianne didn't have to search her mind to realize that helping her pack was another first. Before now, she was always on her own. "Why now?"

Her mother glanced up from shutting the specially made Vuitton case. "What?"

"Why are you finally acting like the mother I always wanted?" Dianne asked.

Lines of irritation radiated across her mother's forehead and at the corner of her mouth. "Dianne, what a question. I think we have everything. The car is waiting."

"It will have to wait until I get an answer," Dianne said. "You and Father basically ignored me all of my life. I would have done anything to have you fuss over me, hug me the way you did tonight, but I never could please either of you."

Her mother blew out an exasperated breath. "I raised you the way my parents raised me. It helped me to be the woman I am today. I'd hoped you would grow up the same way."

"Hoped." Dianne latched on to that one word. "You and Father were ashamed of me until I became the face of Harrington."

"That's a harsh and untrue accusation," her mother flared. "Your father and I are very proud of you. You've shown you have what it takes to keep Harrington House one of the top design houses in the country."

"And coming back will soothe buyers and customers," Dianne said. "You need me to do damage control."

Her mother acted as if she wouldn't answer, but then, "Yes, but it's also what your grandfather wanted."

"You didn't seem to remember that when you let Boswell fire me." Dianne tossed.

"Because we thought it best for the survival of the company," her mother protested.

"The company that ensures that you and Father have a hefty check deposited in your account monthly," Dianne said.

"You've also benefited from the company," her mother quickly pointed out. "We all gain."

"And if there had been no fallout, you wouldn't be here, would you?" Dianne asked. Her mother had the grace to flush.

Dianne was surprised she didn't feel the usual regret, the inadequacies. Her parents didn't love her. She'd finally accepted that. Was she that unlovable? Alex certainly hadn't declared his love. They were great in bed and out, but that didn't mean he loved her. Or did it? There was only one way to find out. "I changed my mind. I'm not going."

Her mother's eyes widened with alarm. "What? You have to come!"

"No, I don't," Dianne said. "You made your choice the day I was fired, and now I've made mine."

"You think he wants you for more than a bed partner, you're wrong," her mother told her tightly. "Alex could have his pick of rich successful women. Why would he want you?"

The hateful words struck home just as her mother had intended. Dianne held her head high, refusing to let her mother know how those words echoed Dianne's worst fear. "Just leave."

"Dianne, don't be foolish." Her mother came to her. "Come with me and you don't have to be dependent on any man. Once you're back at Harrington, you will have the prestige, clout, and money to call the shots. What man wants a woman with nothing? You're little more than a mistress."

Alex had never made her feel that way. He'd made her feel loved, made her dig deep inside herself to be the woman she had always wanted to be, for herself, for him. "You have a car waiting."

Her mother's lips tight, she left. She didn't stop until she was in the entry where her husband and Alex still stood like wary adversaries. "Let's go," she snapped to her husband.

Dianne's father looked from his wife to his daughter. "What happened?"

"I finally stopped trying to do the impossible," Dianne said. "Get you to love me. The price is too high."

"But—" her father began.

"You heard her." Alex opened the door.

Her mother brushed past him. Her husband slowly followed. Alex slammed the door. The vise that had been around his chest when Dianne went to pack slowly loosened its grip. "You all right?"

She lifted her troubled gaze to his. She looked fragile, vulnerable. He cursed under his breath. "What did she say to you?"

Dianne folded her arms. Swallowed. "A number of things actually. It made me realize that we can't go on this way."

Alex felt as if someone had punched him in the gut. He couldn't lose her.

"I have a confession to make," she said softly. "I'd hoped to be in a better position in a few weeks, but my mother made me realize that we need things in the open."

"You're scaring me, Dianne."

She almost smiled. "I'm not at my best, either. My heart is beating like a drum, my knees are shaking."

"Maybe we should both sit down," he suggested.

"I'm not moving from this spot until I'm finished," she said, staring at him intently.

"All right," he said, trying to be patient when he wanted to take her in his arms, hold her, sweep away whatever doubts her mother had created.

She did smile then. "You've always been so patient with me. I could always depend on you. Perhaps, too much."

"Never."

"I shamelessly took advantage of our friendship, and your long habit of always being there when I propositioned you to be my lover," she said.

"And I told you then, if I didn't have feelings for you, I would have walked away," he said, finally going to her. "I'd wanted you for a long time before then. You made a dream come true that I never thought possible. Loving you is what I was born to do." Tears crested in her eyes. He tenderly brushed them away with his thumb. "Please, don't cry. Forget about your parents and act as if they never were here."

She sniffed and shook her head. "That's not possible."

His hands settled gently on her upper forearms. "All right, then. Tell me what's bothering you."

"My mother said you could have your pick of women so why would you want me, that I'm little more than your mistress," she said under her breath. "She's right."

Alex cursed under his breath. "Any man breathing would want you, and we're business partners."

"I'm dependent on you, Alex. We both know if you hadn't rescued me, there is no telling where I would have ended up." She glanced away. "You helped me just like always, and like always, I let you."

"Friends help each other," he told her.

"And that's where we might have a problem," she said, stepping away from him to wrap her slim arms around her waist.

Unease washed over Alex. "I don't understand."

She turned, letting her arms fall to her sides. Her heart thudded in her chest. She was taking a giant risk. She'd finally gotten over her parents' inability to love her; she didn't think there was any hope of accepting Alex not loving her in her lifetime. He was her world. He made life better just with a smile.

"Dianne?" he questioned.

She bit her lip. Was it right of her to tell him her true feelings? If he didn't feel the same, it would embarrass him. They'd be awkward where they'd been carefree and easy around each other. She didn't think she could bear that. "Remember when we started this, you promised you'd always be my friend, no matter what?"

"I remember," he said.

She swallowed. "I'm holding you to that promise."

"Friends no matter what," he said. "I've never broken a promise to you, and I never will."

His reassurance didn't settle her nerves, but it was the best she was going to get. "I want you to know that I didn't mean for this to happen. It came as a surprise, but I wouldn't change it even if I could."

He nodded. "Go on."

She swallowed hard, and pushed the words out. "I love you."

He simply stared at her.

She felt her body began to tremble. "Please don't be mad at me. We can forget what I—"

"Not on your life." Grinning, he came to her. Tenderly his hand cupped her face. "I loved you first with the love of a young boy, then that of a man. I love you, Dianne, with all my heart. With all I am, with all I hope to be."

Tears of joy streamed down her cheeks. Happiness sang in her heart. "Alex, I know I'm not the woman you deserve, but—"

"If you don't want to make me angry, you'll never even think those words again." He stared down into her tearstained eyes. "You're everything that I want. You're loving, bright, caring. You were down, but you got up fighting."

"Because I didn't want to disappoint you. Because I wanted to be worthy of you," she confessed.

"Maybe at first, but I've watched you since you decided what you wanted to do. You're your own woman, you want to succeed on your own," he told her. "You take nothing for granted. You push yourself to succeed." His forehead rested against hers. "Tonight, when you were working on your blog, I was so afraid I was losing you to the business—afraid that you would leave me."

"Never," she said adamantly. Her hands lifted his head. "I could never leave my heart. That's what stopped me. Mother and Father wanted me for their own gain. You want me to be the best I can be for me, and because of that faith, I can be."

"I want to protect you, love you. Luke found out about Boswell's connection to the woman who had replaced you and I notified the board," he told her. "I knew with all the bad press they'd fire him, and your parents might come."

"And you did it anyway?" she asked.

"You'll always come first. I love you, Dianne, with all my heart." He dropped to his knees. "Will you marry me?"

Dianne furiously blinked away the tears in her eyes. She wanted to cherish and remember this moment always. "Yes."

Standing, he pulled her into his arms and kissed her long and hard. "I know women like big weddings that take a lot of time to plan, but I'd like to marry you as soon as possible."

"I can't wait to be your wife."

"You'll never be sorry." He picked her up in his arms. "I'll love you forever."

"I know," she whispered, kissing him on the lips. "Just as I'll always love you. Now take me to bed."

"My pleasure."

Epilogue

Another Bachelor Is Off the Market was the headline for the Fashionista Diva's tweet just before Cicely dragged her tired body off to bed—but not before her avocado facial of course.

Finished with her facial, she looked at all the tweets she'd received asking for more information. Then she switched to the blog.

This afternoon, I was honored to be one of the hundred or so guests for the lavish wedding of designer Dianne Harrington and her business partner and prominent lawyer, Alex Stewart. The ravishing bride wore an off-white long gown with yards of tulle and lace she'd designed for the garden wedding at the beautiful Santa Monica estate of the groom's parents.

The wedding list read like a Who's Who of the business, art, racing, and entertainment worlds. Dianne hit the jackpot with a man who loves her, and an extended family that was warm and personable despite their status.

The official photographs were taken by renowned

photographer Dominique Falcon-Masters. The caterers were overseen by the head chef of the five-star Casa de Serenidad Hotel in Santa Fe, and billionaire Blade and Sierra Navarone's personal chef. Sierra's brother Luke is the groom's brother-in-law.

I'm told only the soothing words of Faith McBride-Grayson, owner of the hotel, and Sierra kept the two highly competitive men from going to war in the kitchen. Noted restaurateur Summer Radcliffe might have been in the kitchen as well if she hadn't been in the wedding party. The food—salmon and châteaubriand—was delicious. The five-foot strawberry-and-lemon wedding cake made me eyes pop, then I moaned with pleasure with my first bite. And, yes, I had another piece. I might have to up my exercise regime for the next month. Although I certainly danced off some of the calories. A certain groomsman might be a bit caveman in his thoughts about his bar, but he was certainly light on his feet.

Sleepy, so I'm signing off. No cameras or cell phones were allowed, but the bride and groom promised I'd have exclusive photos to share within a few days. They wanted to keep the wedding private and intimate—considering the guest list, I can see why.

Until next time, remember: Make fashion your own, don't let fashion own you.

—Diva

William H. Ray

FRANCIS RAY (1944–2013) is the *New York
Times* bestselling author of the Grayson nov-
els, the Falcon books, the Taggart Brothers,
and *Twice the Temptation,* among many
other books. Her novel *Incognito* was made
into a movie that aired on BET. A native
Texan, she was a graduate of Texas Woman's
University and had a degree in nursing. Besides being a writer, she was a school nurse
practitioner with the Dallas Independent
School District. She lived in Dallas.

"Francis Ray is, without a doubt, one of the
Queens of Romance."

—*A Romance Review*

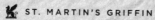